Betsy Was a Junior

Betsy Was a Junior

Maud Hart Lovelace

Illustrated by Vera Neville

📚 HarperTrophy®
An Imprint of HarperCollinsPublishers

Harper Trophy® is a registered trademark of
HarperCollins Publishers Inc.

Betsy Was a Junior
Copyright 1947 by Maud Hart Lovelace
Copyright renewed 1975 by Maud Hart Lovelace
Foreword copyright © 1993 by Anna Quindlen
"Maud Hart Lovelace and Her World" (adapted from *The Betsy-Tacy
Companion: A Biography of Maud Hart Lovelace* by Sharla Scannell Whalen)
copyright © 2000 by HarperCollins Publishers Inc.

LC Number 46-11995
ISBN 0-06-440547-8 (pbk.)
First published by Thomas Y. Crowell Company in 1947.
First Harper Trophy edition, 1995.

Visit us on the World Wide Web!
www.harperchildrens.com

For
BICK, TESS, MIDGE, MARION, EL,
CONNIE, MIL, PAT, *and* RUTH

Contents

Foreword

When I was first asked to speak about Maud Hart Lovelace I had to reread all ten of my Betsy-Tacy books. I would like to make this sound like a hardship, but most of you know better. There are three authors whose body of work I have reread more than once over my adult life: Charles Dickens, Jane Austen, and Maud Hart Lovelace. It was, as always, a pleasure and delight.

And the truth is that I have been preparing for this speech, in a variety of ways, for thirty years, and especially for the last ten. That was the decade in which I began to examine most closely what it meant to be a feminist in America, as I am, and why I felt so strongly that the women's movement and what I believe it stands for has changed my life.

Many of those issues have been explored in my column in *The New York Times*, and over and over again I have tried to reinforce a simple message that I believe has been distorted, muddled, misunderstood, and just plain lied about in recent years by those who want women to go, not forward, but backward.

And that is that feminism is about choices. It is about women choosing for themselves which life roles they wish to pursue. It is about deciding who does and gets and merits and earns and succeeds in what by smarts, capabilities, and heart—not by gender. It is about honoring individuals because of their humanity, not their physiology.

And that is why my theme today is: Betsy Ray, Feminist Icon.

Could there be better books, and could there be a better girl, adolescent, young woman, to teach us all those things about choices than the Betsy-Tacy books and Betsy herself, along with her widely disparate circle of Tacy and Tib, Julia and Margaret, Mrs. Ray and Anna the hired girl, Mrs. Poppy and Miss Mix, Carney and Winona, Miss Bangeter and Miss Clarke? All these different women, who go so many different ways, with false starts and stops, with disappointments and limitations, and yet a sense that they can find a place for themselves in the world.

Do you realize that not once, in any book, does any individual, male or female, suggest to Betsy that she cannot, as she so hopes to do, become a writer? Can anyone possibly appreciate the impact that made on a child like me, wanting it too but seeing all around me on the bookshelves the names of men and seeing all around me in my house the domesticated ways of women?

In the early books, of course, this is not what we see. We see prototypes, really, as surely as Snow White and Rose Red, or Cinderella and her stepsisters. We see three little girls who begin as types: the shy and earnest one; the no-nonsense and literal one; and the ringleader, the storyteller, the adventurer, the center—Elizabeth Warrington Ray. Then the adventures and, more important, the traditions begin—the picnics on the Big Hill, the forays to little Syria, the shopping trips at Christmastime, and Betsy's sheets of foolscap piling up in her Uncle Keith's old trunk.

The books are simply stories of small town life and enduring friendship among little girls, and so it is easy to overlook their importance as teaching tools. But consider the alternatives to children in the early grades. The images of girls tend, overwhelmingly, to be of fairy princesses spinning straw into gold or sleeping until they are awakened by a prince.

Even the best ones usually show us caricatures instead of characters. Recently, for example, I wrote an introduction for a fiftieth anniversary edition of *Madeline* (Viking, 1989). It is one of my favorite picture books for children, has been since I myself was a child, mostly because of one line which sums up the rest of it: "To the tiger in the zoo Madeline just said 'Pooh, pooh.'"

Madeline, unlike the straw-spinning princesses, has attitude. She is nobody's fool.

But attitude, truth to tell, is a surface, two-dimensional characteristic, attractive as it may be. The stories of Betsy, Tacy, and Tib transcend attitude just as the simplistic drawings of the early books give way to the more realistic (albeit, to my mind, slightly oversweet) pictures. They are ultimately books about character, and especially about the character of one girl whose greatest sin, throughout the books, is to undervalue herself.

For those are the mistakes Betsy finds she cannot forgive, when she sells herself short, when she is not all she can be. As opposed to the shy, retiring, and respectful girl who became so valued in girl's fiction, Betsy does best when she serves herself, when she is true to herself. In this she most resembles two other fictional heroines who, not surprisingly, also long to be writers and take their work very seriously indeed. One is Anne Shirley of the *Anne of Green Gables* books, and the other is Jo March of *Little Women*.

But the key difference, I think, is a critical one. Both Anne and Jo are implicitly made to pay in those books for the fact that they do not conform to feminine norms. Anne begins life as an orphan and never is permitted to forget that she must work for a living—in fact, you might call her the Joe Willard of girls, although she is far less prickly and far more easy to like than Joe Willard. Jo March of *Little Women* habitually reminds herself how unattractive she is and settles down, in one of the most unconvincing matches in fiction, with the older, most unromantic Professor Bhaer. It is her beautiful sister Amy who gets the real guy, the rich and romantic Laurie.

* * *

Betsy, by contrast, never had to pay for the sin of being herself; in fact, she only finds herself under a cloud when she is less than herself. At base, she is a charmed soul from beginning to end because she can laugh at herself and take herself seriously at the same time, because she is serious but never a prig, and interested in boys but never a flirt. Can anyone forget the moment when, returning from the sophomore dance at Schiller Hall with that absolute poop Phil Brandish trying to worm his fist into her pocket, she turns to him with desperation and blurts out, "You might as well know. I don't hold hands."

In fact it's probably in that book, *Betsy in Spite of Herself*, that we see Betsy most the way I think we were always meant to see her, as a girl who will do what is right for her, not necessarily what the world wants her to do. But first, like most of us, she has to do what is wrong for her to find out what is right. She decides to nab Phil just for the fun of it, and to that end she adds the letter E to the end of her perfectly good name, sprays herself with Jockey Club perfume, and uses green stationery to write notes instead of her poetry or stories. It's inevitable—when the real Betsy sneaks out, in the form of a song parody she and Tacy invented before the Phil/Betsy affair began, they break up. But instead of a sore heart, Betsy is left with Shakespeare: "This above all: to thine own self be true."

Betsy already knows, as do we, that that self varies widely from girl to girl, that there is no little box that will fit them all. In *Heaven to Betsy*, she says, in the passage that made the future so clear and yet so mysterious for me:

> She had been almost appalled, when she started going around with Carney and Bonnie, to discover how fixed and definite their ideas of marriage were. They both had cedar hope chests and took pleasure in embroidering their initials on towels to lay away. Each one had picked out a silver pattern and they were planning to give each other spoons in these patterns for Christmases and birthdays. When Betsy and Tacy and Tib talked about their future they planned to be writers, dancers, circus acrobats.

Betsy never looks down on those aspirations of Carney and Bonnie's. But she never looks away from her own aspirations. She follows a sensible progression from writing, to dreaming of being a writer, to actually saying she is going to be one, to sending her stories (when she is a mere senior in high school) to various women's magazines. She makes the mistake so many of us make—like Jo in *Little Women*, she learns early on that writing about debutantes in Park Avenue penthouses is doomed to failure if you've neither debuted nor visited Park Avenue—but her gumption carries her through.

And there are, interestingly, no naysayers among her

family members. While the Rays have three daughters, early on two of them are already committed to having careers outside the home, Julia as an opera singer, Betsy as a writer. Betsy's parents are totally committed to this idea for them both, sending Julia to the Twin Cities and even to Europe to further her training as a singer, and arguing vociferously that Betsy's work is as good as any that appears in popular magazines.

The idea of something that is yours to do became narrower and narrower as my mother grew up. As Betty Friedan wrote in *The Feminine Mystique* (Dell, 1963), by the time my mother was ready to enter what Julia always called The Great World, it had narrowed to one role and one role alone, that of wife and mother.

I don't know when exactly I knew that that was never going to be enough for me. But I know where I got the idea that more was possible. It wasn't from career women or role models—when I was a girl, there really weren't any.

I learned it from books, and none more than from the stories about Betsy, Tacy, and Tib. Because the most important thing about Betsy Ray is that she has a profound sense of confidence and her own worth.

Of course, if this had been wrapped in a sanctimonious, plaster saint package, Betsy would have been—perish the thought—Elsie Dinsmore, the perfect, boring little girl of popular fiction who Betsy herself once mocks. And, if there had been no boys in the books, I, for one, wouldn't have read them.

But we did read them, many of us, for so many reasons: because Maud Hart Lovelace had a real gift for adapting the prose to the appropriate age level, and the themes, too; because we fell in love, not only with Betsy but with Tacy and Tib and all the others, and wanted to know from year to year what was happening to them; because of Magic Wavers and Sunday night sandwiches and smoky coffee brewed out of doors and all the other little ordinary things that, in some fashion, became our ordinary things.

And because they were just like us.

But we know there are many us's, with many different goals and aspirations. For many years those goals and aspirations were truncated by one simple fact: our sex. Everything around us reflected that, from who sat on the Supreme Court, to who listened to our chests when we were sick, to who oversaw services when we went to church on Sunday.

But from time to time we encountered a teacher, or a parent, or even a book that told us that we should let our ambitions fly, that we should believe in ourselves, that the only limits we should put on what we tried for were the limits of our desires and our talents. When I told people I was going to give this speech, most had never heard of

Betsy-Tacy, and I had to describe them as a series of books for girls. But they were so much more than that to one little girl who grew up to be a woman writer and who, perhaps, learned that she *could* by the example given inside these books.

—ANNA QUINDLEN

(Adapted from a speech given to the Twin Cities Chapter of the Betsy-Tacy Society on June 12, 1993)

"Haste thee nymph, and bring with thee Jest and Youthful Jollity . . ."

—JOHN MILTON

1

Taking Stock

BETSY RAY SAT IN a rowboat which was anchored in
Babcock's Bay, two watery miles opposite Murmuring Lake Inn, where the Ray family had been spending the summer. The oars were folded across the boat
and on the seat beside her lay a fat notebook which
she used as a journal and several sharply pointed pencils. She sat with her arms bound about her knees,

staring at a gauzy-winged dragon fly which had come to rest on the prow of the boat. Her expression was serious, not to say grim. She was taking stock.

Betsy was fond of this bay. It was strewn thickly with water lilies. Their flat green pads and creamy, richly scented blossoms floated on the water all around her. The shore was lined with trees—willows, cottonwoods, box elders. In other parts of the lake rows of summer cottages or low-lying farms came to the water's edge. This cove was remote; moored here, you might have thought that you were in a wilderness except for the fact that a green wooded point, jutting into the lake to the east, showed the rooftop of the Inn.

When Betsy wished to achieve the illusion of a wilderness she did not look in that direction.

Murmuring Lake Inn was a highly social place. Crowds of young people followed a careless routine —walks, boat rides, and leisurely games of croquet; bathing every afternoon at four. Mothers rocked, read and embroidered on the shady porches and vacationing fathers fished. Mr. Ray drove out from his shoe store in nearby Deep Valley every night, and in the evening there were launch rides and informal hops in the big parlor.

Betsy had had a gay summer. She was sorry it was ending tomorrow. She wondered now, staring at the dragon fly, and beyond him across the glassy lake, whether it had been too gay, but decided that it hadn't been.

"It's been wonderful," she thought. "It's just the sort of summer you ought to have at sixteen."

Betsy was sixteen and next month she would begin her third year of high school. She was exactly halfway through, which made this an excellent time for taking stock.

"I wish I was just beginning and had it all ahead of me," she said with a long romantic sigh. But she said it because she thought it was the proper thing to say. She was really pleased to be an upper classman.

She had certainly had fun. She belonged to a flexible Crowd of a dozen or so boys and girls who stirred up fun as briskly as the cook at the Inn stirred up hot cakes for breakfast. She had really been too frivolous, Betsy decided. Yet the two years had had their perplexities, too, their worries, and even their heartaches.

She had had heartaches over boys, over wanting to be popular. The Ray house, with its three daughters, was always full of boys but boys liked Betsy usually in a friendly sort of way. She had longed to be a siren like her older sister, Julia.

In particular, during her freshman year, she had had a heartache over Tony. Although a classmate, he was slightly older, more sophisticated than the rest. He had a bush of curly black hair, bold laughing eyes, a lazy drawling voice. Betsy had thought she was in love with him, but he had only liked her in a maddening, brotherly way. By the end of the year, however, her infatuation had ebbed away. She liked Tony still, almost better than any boy she knew, but now her feeling was as sisterly as his was brotherly.

"That's life for you," Betsy said aloud, and appropriately, the dragon fly flew away.

In her freshman year, too, she had had a heartache over losing the Essay Contest. Every year the two societies into which the school was divided competed for a cup in essay writing. Both years Betsy had been chosen to represent her class and both years she had lost to Joe Willard. He was an orphan who was working his way through school. Betsy liked him very much but she didn't like losing the Essay Contest.

She had minded it most the first year, for then she had felt guilty. She had not prepared for the Contest properly, she had not read the material she was supposed to have read. One of the great lessons she had learned in high school had come after that defeat. She had learned that her gift for writing was important to her and that she must never neglect it.

"I haven't really neglected it since," she thought. "I've kept up my journal, I'm writing a novel, I worked hard on my English assignments last year and I studied for the Essay Contest. I lost it again but this time it wasn't through any fault of mine."

She had not done her best because, by an ironical chance, the Contest had coincided with a quarrel she had had with Phil Brandish.

Phil Brandish had been the great outstanding triumph of Betsy's sophomore year. She had tried that year to acquire a new personality, to act Dramatic and Mysterious, and in this role she had captured Phil Brandish's interest. But she had not enjoyed pretending all the time to be something she wasn't. She had decided before the season ended that she preferred, usually, just to be herself.

"I learned a lot from that affair, though," she thought now, frowning. "I've had more poise with boys since then. Julia says I'm more charming. Of course, I didn't keep Phil, but then, I didn't want to."

He was a sulky, aloof boy whose chief charm had been a red automobile. He and his twin, Phyllis, were grandchildren of the rich Home Brandish, who lived in a mansion on the west side of Deep Valley. Phyllis went to boarding school—Browner Seminary in Milwaukee. By a coincidence this school was attended by a great friend of Betsy's, Thelma Muller, irrevocably nicknamed Tib.

Betsy's oldest and closest friend was red-haired

Tacy Kelly. They had been loyal, loving chums since Betsy's fifth birthday party. And they had been friends with Tib almost as long as they had been friends with each other. Tib was tiny, yellow-headed, as daring as she was pretty. Betsy and Tacy loved to think up adventurous things to do, but it had usually been Tib who did them. She had lived in a large chocolate-colored house. She could dance. She had exquisite clothes. Even when she was their daily companion, Tib had been a figure of romance to Betsy and Tacy.

And when they were all in the eighth grade, she had moved away to Milwaukee.

Last year Betsy had gone to spend Christmas with her. The visit to the big foreign-flavored city, the glimpse into Tib's life, with its sheltered private school, its encircling *Grosspapas* and *Grossmamas,* uncles, aunts and cousins, had been an illuminating experience. It was while visiting there that Betsy had decided to become Dramatic and Mysterious. The visit had had a thrilling ending for on New Year's Eve Tib had told her that the family might move back to Deep Valley.

"I wonder whether she really will come some day," Betsy thought. A breeze had sprung up, ruffling the water and bringing a faint, not unpleasantly fishy smell. The boat rocked dreamily.

Betsy roused herself, reached for her journal. Wetting

her pencil with the tip of her tongue she began to write.

"I'm going to make my junior year just perfect," she wrote. "In the first place I'm going to stay around home a lot. Julia is going off to the University and Papa and Mamma and Margaret will all miss her terribly—almost as much as I will."

It wasn't that Julia had ever helped much around the house, Betsy thought, lowering her pencil. Anna, the Rays' hired girl, was so efficient that there wasn't much need for any of the daughters to help. But Julia was so loving and vital. Her personality filled the house just as her music did. Julia planned to be an opera singer and was playing and singing all day long. She played popular music, too, for the Crowd to sing.

"I resolve next," Betsy continued writing, "to learn to play the piano. The family has always wanted me to take piano lessons and I've always dodged them. But with Julia going I'll just have to learn. I can't imagine our house without music. I'll start taking lessons and practise an hour every day if it kills me. (It probably will.)

"In school," she went on, "I want my year to be completely wonderful. I hope I'll be elected a class officer again. And I'd like to head up a committee for the junior-senior banquet. That's the most important event of the junior year. Above all I want another try at the Essay Contest. I want that terribly. I think I'll have it, too. And I'm really going to study. I'm going to try to get good marks. I've never done my best."

She read over what she had written, suffused by a warm virtuous glow.

"As for boys," Betsy concluded, and her writing grew very firm and black, *"I think I'll go with Joe Willard!"*

She emphasized this declaration with an exclamation point and some heavy underlining, which was fitting. It was really the keystone of the structure she had built. Unconsciously, perhaps, she had figured out just what kind of a girl she thought Joe Willard would like, and that was the kind she was planning to be.

He didn't have money to spend on girls. He couldn't afford frivolity. When he started going around with a girl, she would surely be the kind Betsy had just described—one who was devoted to her home, who gave her spare time to some worth while thing like music, a leader in school.

But it would take planning to go with him, no matter how admirable she made herself. Unfortunately, Joe Willard didn't seem to want girls in his life. It was because of his shortage of money, Betsy felt sure.

"But I can make him see that money doesn't matter,"

she planned. "I'll just have to lure him up to the house." Once a boy came to the merry, hospitable Ray house he almost always came again.

It was pleasant to sit in a gently rocking boat, listening to killdees on the shore, and think about going with Joe Willard. Betsy had liked him for several years now. She had met him the summer before she entered high school, in the little hamlet of Butternut Center where he was clerking in his uncle's store. She was on her way home, after visiting on a farm, and he had sold her some presents to take to her family, and Tacy.

During the two years of high school a series of small misunderstandings had kept them apart, but he liked her, Betsy felt sure, just as she liked him.

"Not in a silly way," she thought. "We're just going to be wonderful, wonderful friends—for the present, that is," she added hastily. She was quite aware that it would be easy to be romantic about Joe Willard. He was so extremely good looking with light hair cut in a pompadour, and blue eyes under thick golden brows. His red lower lip protruded recklessly. He was not downed by the fact that he had no home, no parents and very little money.

"He'll have more money this year," Betsy thought. He had planned, she knew, to work with a threshing rig all summer, following the harvest northward. He had expected to earn three dollars a day and save it for his expenses during the coming school year.

"I suppose he'll work after school at the creamery again. That won't matter. He'll be able to come to see me sometimes, and we'll talk by the hour. How he'll love Papa's Sunday night lunches, and the way Mamma plays for us to dance!"

She sat still for a moment smiling at the distant chimney of the Inn as though it were Joe Willard.

When she smiled, Betsy's face lighted with a charm of which she was quite unaware. She didn't like her square white teeth which were, in her own phrase "parted in the middle." But her smile, quick and very bright, gave a hint of her response to life which was trusting and joyful.

She was a tall, slender girl with soft brown hair worn in a pompadour over a "jimmy." It was wavy now, but only because it had been wound the night before on Magic Wavers. She had dark-lashed hazel eyes, and a pink and white skin. This she prized mightily. It was, she considered, her only claim to beauty, and Betsy worshipped beauty.

If a fairy godmother had ever appeared in her vicinity waving a wand and offering favors, Betsy would have cried out unhesitatingly for beauty. Her favorite daydream was of suddenly becoming beautiful with "bright hair streaming down" like the Lily

Maid of Astolot's, or dark raven tresses.

The members of her Crowd sometimes exchanged "trade lasts"—T.L.s, they were called. A "trade last" was a compliment, heard about another person, repeated to him after he had first repeated a compliment heard about you. Betsy was always being told for a T.L. that she had been described as interesting, sweet or charming. It infuriated her.

"I want to be pretty!" she stormed to Tacy.

"You're better than pretty," Tacy answered sometimes and Betsy would respond inelegantly, "Pooh for that!"

After smiling for a long time at the chimney which was masquerading as Joe Willard, she slapped her notebook shut, put it back on the seat and took up the oars. Instinct told her it was almost four o'clock. Betsy often rowed over to Babcock's Bay in the early afternoon, which was "nap time" at the Inn. She liked to be alone sometimes to read, write on her novel, or just think. But she always got back for the bathing.

Slipping the oars into the water, she turned the boat about. She rowed unskillfully, her oars churned up showers of glittering drops, but she sent the heavy boat hurrying over the water.

2

Making Plans

THE LONG INN DOCK was lined with boats and draped with fishnets. Old Pete, smoking his pipe in the lee of the boathouse, hobbled forward with rheumatic slowness to pull Betsy in. She stepped out cautiously, the boat rocking beneath her feet, and lingered to talk with him. They were great friends. He sometimes told her stories about when her mother was a girl and lived at Pleasant Park across the lake.

"She was a handsome redhead. I used to see her out in her sailboat, 'The Queen of the Lake.' Her brother Keith would be with her, the one who ran away to be an actor. He was redheaded, too, and as handsome as they come."

"He's still an actor. He's with Mr. Otis Skinner this season in *The Honor of the Family*," Betsy had answered, glowing. Her mother's brother, Keith Warrington, was very close to Betsy although she had seen him only once.

She used his old theatrical trunk for a desk. She kept her manuscripts, notebooks and pencils in the tray, and wrote on the smooth top with pleasure, feeling that in some intangible way the storied background, the venturesome travels of the trunk added magic to her pencil. The trunk had come to represent her writing, her dearest plans for her life.

Old Pete said now only that there was going to be a change in the weather.

"This gloriously perfect summer can't last forever," answered Betsy. She ran up a steep flight of stairs, which spanned the high bank through a tangled growth of bushes and trees.

At the top she was greeted by a delicious smell from the Inn kitchens—baking cake, she thought. A clothes line hung full of bathing suits and stockings.

Betsy selected her own and paused at the pump which stood at one end of the porch just outside Mrs. Van Blarcum's office.

Mrs. Van Blarcum was small, spare, vivacious, always busy from morning until night. Mr. Van Blarcum was courtly, with drooping white mustaches, always leisurely. They had operated the Inn for many years and the same families returned summer after summer from Deep Valley and other Minnesota towns, as well as from Iowa, the Dakotas, Nebraska, Kansas and Missouri.

The Inn was old. It had received so many additions at different periods that it had quite lost its original shape and sprawled in strange directions, unified only by white paint and a narrow open porch across the front.

Guests overflowed the main building and slept in cottages. These ranged in an uneven semicircle among old apple trees around the smooth green lawn. The Rays had the cottage on the end of the point. It consisted only of two bedrooms with a porch in front. Unplastered, it smelled freshly of the lake which could be seen in a rippling silver sheet through the foliage outside the windows.

The three sisters occupied one bedroom. Julia and Margaret were there putting on their bathing suits, when Betsy dashed in. The bathing suits were all of heavy blue serge, trimmed with white braid around the sailor collars, the elbow-length sleeves, and the skirts which came to the knee over ample bloomers. With them the girls wore long black stockings and neatly laced canvas oxfords. Julia was tying a red bandana around her dark hair.

She was a beautiful girl with violet eyes, a classic nose, and white teeth which, unlike Betsy's, were conventionally spaced. She was shorter than Betsy, but made the most of every inch of height, longing to be tall because of her operatic ambitions.

"How's the novel going?" she asked Betsy, adjusting the ends of her kerchief artfully and looking in a hand mirror to see the effect.

"I wasn't working on that today; just writing in my journal. I'm making wonderful plans for next year. Gee, it seems funny to be an upper classman!"

"It doesn't seem a bit funny to me to be finished," Julia said. "In fact I feel as though I should have finished long ago. Eighteen years of my life gone and I haven't yet got down to music in a serious way! Come here, Margaret dear," she added to the younger sister, "and I'll tie your bandana."

"Yoo hoo, Betsy!" came voices from outside.

"No matter where we live or go," Julia said, laughing, "there's always someone yoo-hooing outside for you, Bettina."

This was true, and Betsy liked to hear it.

"There's been a grand crowd out here this summer," she replied, scrambling into her suit.

She had enjoyed getting acquainted with people from other places. There were two boys her own age from Deep Valley too. Betsy looked for them now as, tying her kerchief hurriedly, she rushed out the door.

Dave Hunt had already run down the stairs. He ignored girls and usually went fishing with the men. Yet his presence had added an extra fillip to the summer, for now and then Betsy found him staring at her out of deep-set dark blue eyes. He was over six feet tall and very thin, with a stern, spare face.

E. Lloyd Harrington was highly social. He, too, was tall, but fragile. He had beautiful manners and loved to dance. He usually wore glasses and was blinking now without them.

Julia was joined by Roger Tate, a University student. For a week he had been trailing her, talking about the U, as he called it, and making plans for the days following her arrival there. He was going to take her, Julia told Betsy, to a fraternity dance—whatever that was; riverbanking—that meant walking along the Mississippi, he explained; to lunch in Minneapolis tea rooms. He was teaching her to swim.

"Today I want you to go as far as the buoy," he said.

"I'll try." Julia lifted her violet eyes, smiled with intention. Roger blushed and began to talk hurriedly, almost senselessly, about side strokes and breast strokes. Betsy shook her head. She had seen plenty of Julia's conquests and they always amused and interested her. But she didn't like it at the end when Julia threw her victims over.

Dave went so far out into the lake that Old Pete blew a horn and summoned him back. Betsy could swim only a little, but she had fun with water wings and floated a long time, looking up into the blue world of the sky, thinking about next winter.

At five o'clock everyone went dripping back to his room to dress for supper.

A day at Murmuring Lake Inn did not have one climax; it had three: the three superb meals. Guests rose from the enormous breakfast swearing that they could never eat again. Yet they were waiting hungrily on the porches when the dinner bell rang. And although the noon meal was abundant beyond all reason, everyone was waiting shamelessly for the supper bell.

The Ray girls and their mother waited on the porch of their cottage. Julia and Betsy had changed into white dotted swiss dresses, Margaret into a yellow sailor suit. Mrs. Ray wore crisp pale green trimmed with bands of plaid.

"Papa's late tonight," she said. "He's almost always here by now."

An inadvertent tinkle sounded as one of the maids came out on the porch carrying a big brass bell. Before she had a chance to ring it guests started streaming toward the dining room. She swung it heartily and the loud metallic clangor caused those guests who were housed in cottages to start from their porches, except for the Rays.

"I'm starving," Betsy said.

"So am I," answered Mrs. Ray. "But it isn't civilized not to wait for Papa."

"At least three minutes," Julia said.

"There he is now," Margaret said.

Sure enough, a fringed surrey had stopped at the far side of the Inn, and Mr. Ray alighted.

"Why, he's helping somebody out," said Mrs. Ray. "I wonder who it can be."

Curiosity born of their quiet days sent them hurrying over the lawn.

They saw a small, golden-haired figure, very chic in a high-waisted, lilac-sprigged dress. Betsy stared. Then she shrieked. Then she began to run.

"Tib!" she cried. "Tib Muller!"

She and Tib flung their arms about each other.

"Where did you come from?"

"I rode out from Deep Valley with your father."

"But you belong in Milwaukee."

"No," said Tib. "We've moved back. I live in Deep Valley now. I'm going to go to the Deep Valley High School right along with you and Tacy."

They looked into each other's eyes, almost tearful with joy. Then Tib embraced Mrs. Ray, Julia and Margaret.

"Take her to Mrs. Van Blarcum and get her a room," said Mr. Ray, looking pleased with himself. He was a tall, dark-haired man, with hazel eyes like Betsy's.

Hand in hand, in a quiver of excitement, Betsy and Tib ran to Mrs. Van Blarcum. The room must be big enough for Betsy, too, they insisted, hugging each other; they refused to be separated. They reached the supper table late, but by this time they had quieted down enough to remember that they were sixteen, and they walked demurely across the dining room.

Mrs. Van Blarcum had put a chair for Tib at the Ray family table. Everyone was happily agitated by her arrival.

"When did you get back?" Mrs. Ray asked, as Betsy and Tib helped themselves liberally to crisply-fried lake fish, cottage-fried potatoes, stewed fresh tomatoes, green corn on the cob, cold slaw and muffins still warm to the touch.

"Just yesterday," said Tib. "Mamma and Matilda

are very busy settling, but they said I might come out when Mr. Ray invited me. I was so anxious to see Betsy." She spoke with a slight foreign inflection, a result of the years in Milwaukee with her German relatives.

"Have you seen Tacy?" asked Julia.

"Yes," said Tib. "I went up to her house last night. I could hardly believe it, how tall and grown-up she was. But after I had talked with her a minute I could see that she hadn't changed."

"Tacy is always the same."

"Margaret has changed, though," said Tib, smiling at Betsy's younger sister. "You're ten years old now, aren't you, Margaret?"

"Yes," said Margaret, looking up gravely out of large blue eyes, heavily lashed with black.

"Margaret has braids," said Betsy, lifting one.

They were short, but that didn't matter, for they were almost completely concealed by giant hair bows behind each ear, yellow tonight, to match the sailor suit.

"You're just Hobbie's age," said Tib, referring to her brother. She had two brothers, Frederick and Hobson. "You'll have to come up and play with him."

"Thank you," said Margaret politely, but the Rays knew that she was quite unlikely to accept the invitation. Margaret didn't play very much, even with girls.

She liked books, and Washington, her cat, and Abe Lincoln, her dog, and the company of grown-ups, especially a neighbor, Mrs. Wheat. She liked to be with her father and went with him on walks and rambles, always holding his hand and standing very straight as he did. The Persian Princess, her sisters called her.

Blaming the lake air, they emptied a plateful of muffins. It was filled again. For dessert stewed plums were served with Lady Baltimore cake. There were coffee and tea, both iced and hot, and big pitchers of milk.

Betsy stole a look around the crowded, clattering dining room. She was gratified to see that Dave Hunt was looking at her as usual. He looked away when she met his eyes. Lloyd was staring frankly at Tib, and as soon as supper was over he joined them to be introduced. All the boys and girls came except Dave.

Tib was gracious, a trifle flustered. She laughed all the time, a little tinkling laugh which sounded exactly as she looked. Betsy remembered having recommended such a laugh during her visit to Milwaukee.

It was on New Year's Eve. They had stayed awake all night planning new personalities, and Betsy had resolved to be Dramatic and Mysterious. Tib, they had decided, should be the silly type. She was really practical and exceptionally competent, but Betsy had declared that she must conceal it if she wanted to fascinate boys. Betsy had long since stopped acting Dramatic and Mysterious, but Tib was still acting adorably silly with very good effect.

Lloyd stared at her admiringly behind his glasses. He proposed getting Pete to take them all out in the launch. As they went chug-chugging into the lake, spreading ruffles of foam in the sunset-tinted water, he sat next to Tib.

When they returned he talked with Mrs. Van Blarcum and proudly announced a hop. Betsy was puzzled.

"But I thought there wasn't going to be one tonight. So many people are making an early start tomorrow."

"Plans have been changed. Guess why!" said Lloyd.

Tib laughed her little tinkling laugh and Betsy whispered, hugging her, "What you're going to do to the Deep Valley High School!"

Impromptu though it was, the hop was a success. Mrs. Ray and another mother alternated at the piano. Mrs. Ray knew only two dance tunes, a waltz and a two-step, but she played them over and over, and with such zest that they eclipsed in popularity the more extensive repertoire of the other mother.

Tib flashed from boy to boy. Betsy had plenty of partners, too. Julia danced most of the evening with

Roger, looking pensive, presumably because they must now be parted until the University opened its doors.

At last Mrs. Ray played "Good Night Ladies," Mrs. Van Blarcum served lemonade, and Betsy and Tib could get away.

Tib's room was on the second floor of the hotel. It was plainly furnished, as all the Inn rooms were, but with a drift of white towels on the wash stand and snowy linen on the bed. It smelled of the lake, and the girls were delighted to find that it had its own small balcony.

"We'll go out there and talk," Betsy cried, "as soon as we're ready for bed."

They put gaily patterned kimonos over their night-gowns. Tib tied her yellow curls with a ribbon and Betsy wound her hair on Magic Wavers. Then they went stealthily outside, sat down on the floor and looked upward.

Clouds had come into the sky; you could see the stars only through ragged holes. The tops of the apple trees stirred above the small dark cottages. Crickets were singing.

"How did you get along with your new personality after you got home?" Tib asked.

"Well, I took Phil Brandish's scalp," answered Betsy. "I got tired, though, of not being myself."

"I thought you didn't act very Dramatic and Mysterious tonight."

"I put it on when I want to. It's useful to know how. But as a regular thing I prefer to be myself. You were doing a grand job of acting silly, Tib."

"Yes. I laugh all the time when I'm around boys, just like you told me to."

"How does it work?"

"Fine. I didn't know many boys in Milwaukee, but I met some on the train and they seemed perfectly fascinated. It annoys Mamma. She keeps saying that I make such a false impression."

"Which is *just* what you're trying to do!"

They rocked with hushed laughter.

Betsy told Tib about the plans she had made in Babcock's Bay, how she was going to triumph in school that year and that she expected to go with Joe Willard. Tib listened raptly.

"You'll like Joe," Betsy said. "He's not only the handsomest boy I know, but he has so much character. Just think of him putting himself through school!"

"He sounds wonderful," said Tib. "I'm sure he's just the one for you, Betsy. Who shall I go with?"

"We'll pick out someone grand."

"It's going to be fun going to high school." Tib put her arm around Betsy. "I loved Browner and hated to leave it, but it will be thrilling to be in a school with you and Tacy—and boys."

The next morning the sky was overcast. Treetops were lost in mist. The chairs lining the Inn porches were too wet to sit down in, although there had been no rain.

The Rays and Tib packed grips and stowed them into the surrey. Good-byes flew over the green lawn, along the narrow porches. Mr. Van Blarcum, looking courtly, and Mrs. Van Blarcum, looking harried, followed them out to the carriage.

Roger looked melancholy. "I'll meet your train if you'll let me know when you expect to arrive at Minneapolis," he said to Julia.

Lloyd smiled at Tib. "We've just bought a new auto. How about a ride when I get back to Deep Valley?"

Tib gave an enchanting little giggle. "Maybe. I'm afraid of autos," said Tib, who was afraid of nothing.

Lloyd gave Betsy only an absent handclasp but she didn't mind, for from the outskirts of the crowd Dave was looking at her out of his deep-set eyes.

"If I weren't going to go with Joe this year, I'd try to make that Dave Hunt talk. I really would," thought Betsy.

3
Introducing the Crowd

THE RAY HOME STOOD AT the corner of High Street and Plum, facing on High which ran horizontally along one of Deep Valley's many hills. High was a broad leafy street full of comfortable homes. Two blocks from the Rays the red brick high school lifted its turreted roofs, and on top of the Hill stood the German Catholic College, a grey pile with a look of the old world about it. The nuns offered classes in English as well as in German, and Tacy's sister Katie was enrolled there for the fall term.

The Ray house was painted green, and although obviously new, it had a homelike look. Vines climbed the walls. There were bridal wreath and hydrangea bushes on the lawn, and hanging baskets filled with flowers festooned the small square porch.

This porch didn't look natural in the summer time without boys and girls perched on the steps and railings. Inside, too, the house seemed most like itself with a gay young crowd around. The piano, the center of everything, stood in a square entrance hall from which the golden oak staircase ascended. Julia always called this hall the music room.

The day the family returned from the lake Betsy's Crowd arrived in force. Tony Markham lounged in first. He tried to act nonchalant about their return but the affection he felt for them all shone in his big black eyes. He sat down on the couch and Betsy and Julia sat on either side of him, with Margaret cross-legged on the floor in front.

"Hi!" he called to Mrs. Ray. "Call off your daughters, can't you?"

"But we're glad to see you, Tony," the girls protested.

"Heck, I'll bet you never thought of me all summer!"

He gave Margaret a souvenir he had brought back

for her from his own vacation to Chicago, a metal teddy bear holding a red pin cushion in its arms.

"I'll keep it on my bureau," Margaret said, her small face crinkling in delight. Tony was her special favorite.

He strolled out to the kitchen to see Anna, who turned from the oven, smiling. She wore a clean coverall apron; her hair was twisted into a tight knot above her broad face. She too had been away on a vacation, to the Twin Cities.

"I saw your Charlie. He looked lonesome," Tony said.

"Ja, he was lonesome. He wants me to get married, Charlie does."

"Oh, Anna!" cried Betsy. "Are you going to?"

"Na, I'm not much on the marrying. Mrs. McCloskey used to say to me, 'Anna, why don't you marry Charlie? He's got such a good job as barkeep down at the Corner Café. He'd be a good provider.' But I'd say, 'Na, Mrs. McCloskey, I'd rather cook for you.'"

"And now you'd rather cook for us, wouldn't you, Anna?" asked Betsy, squeezing her arm. "Aren't we nicer than the McCloskeys?"

"Don't bother me now," said Anna, who wouldn't be disloyal either to the Rays or to the distant, perhaps fictional McCloskeys. "Go away and I'll have hot cookies for you in a minute."

Before the cookies were ready more visitors had come—Tom Slade, who hadn't yet left for the military school which he attended; Dennis Farisy, who had curly hair and a dimple in his chin; Cab Edwards, his boon companion. Cab lived just behind the Rays, a spruce smiling boy with shiny black hair. His father owned a furniture store, in which Cab had been working during vacation.

Tacy only telephoned from Tib's house but Alice Morrison, Winona Root and Irma Biscay came together. Irma had large soft eyes and a rounded figure, and although she made no effort, seemingly, to attract boys, she drew them as clover does bees. Other girls might lack a beau for long periods or short, but never, never Irma.

Winona was tall and dashing. There was an irrepressible gleam in her eyes, mischief in the white flash of her smile. Alice, as blonde as Winona was dark, was more sedate. She had to be; her parents were strict.

"Kids! Kids!" Carney Sibley rushed in, showing her dimple. She had a dimple in her left cheek only and the effect was piquant. Carney wore glasses but her prettiness triumphed over glasses. She was a senior, a frank, forthright girl, enormously popular with both boys and girls.

"What is it? What's the matter?" The Crowd started up.

"Come on out and look! Papa's bought an automobile!"

They rushed out the front door and a Buick was, indeed, standing at the hitching post where Phil Brandish's machine was wont to stand last year. Mr. Sibley, smiling broadly, sat behind the wheel.

Mr. Ray and Margaret hurried out, too.

"Where's Dandy?" Margaret wanted to know. Dandy was the Sibley's horse.

"He's gone to the country to live with my uncle," Carney said. She glanced slyly at her father. "We can't forget him though. Papa says 'Giddap!' when he wants the auto to go faster and 'Whoa!' when he wants it to stop."

Margaret slipped her hand into her father's, and Betsy knew she felt lonesome for Dandy. Her own heart yearned briefly toward the old bay horse who had driven the Crowd all over the county on endless high jinks. But the new automobile with its brass lamps, the high seats padded and upholstered in leather, was fetching indeed.

"I'm going to learn to drive it and then I'll take you all out riding," Carney said.

Her father drove away, but Carney remained to eat cookies and hear about Tib. Betsy had told the great news that Tib was back for keeps in Deep Valley. Alice, Winona and Tom remembered her. The others knew her only from Betsy's rhapsodic descriptions.

"Is she really as nifty as you say?" demanded Cab.

"Niftier," Betsy declared. "She came out to the lake with Papa last night, and you should have seen her bowl Lloyd Harrington over."

"When is Lord Byron Edwards going to meet her?"

"What about Casanova Farisy?"

"Neither of you has a chance," drawled Tony, sticking his thumbs in his vest. "Get out of the way, boys!"

Irma's laughter was appreciative of this wit.

"Maybe she'll come to my party. It's for girls only, though. I'm giving a party for Phyllis Brandish, Betsy." Irma had gone out with Phil frequently since he and Betsy had quarreled the previous spring.

"Do you know, Betsy," Winona asked, "that Phyllis is coming here to school?"

"How nice! Maybe she'll go with our Crowd." But Betsy said that only to sound casual. Personally, she thought Phyllis Brandish was too worldly for their Crowd. She didn't really like Phil's sister.

Julia came in just then and sat down at the piano. She began to play, and the Crowd, as though at a signal, hooked arms and formed a semicircle behind her. There were some good voices, Tony's deep bass, Dennie's tenor, Betsy's soft alto, Irma's sweet soprano. They missed Tacy, whose voice had a vibrant heart-stirring quality. Tacy had temperament, Julia always said.

> *"School days, school days,*
> *Dear old golden rule days. . . ."*

They sang ardently, and

> *"San Antoni . . . Antonio,*
> *She hopped upon a pony,*
> *And ran away with Tony. . . ."*

Tony seized Betsy and galloped madly around the music room to show how it was done.

It was a typical gathering of the Crowd, but there wasn't another for several days. Until school began Betsy spent every waking moment at the Mullers'.

They had moved back into their chocolate-colored house, near Tacy's in the Hill Street neighborhood. It was large, with a tower in one corner and a pane of colored glass over the front door. In their childhood Betsy and Tacy had thought it the most beautiful house in the world.

It gave Betsy a queer feeling, such as you get from hearing a strain of old music or from smelling a perfume associated with bygone days to see the blue velvet furniture back in the Mullers' round front parlor, to smell coffee cake baking in Matilda's shining kitchen, and to watch Mr. Muller sipping beer.

Tacy, too, was happy and excited over Tib's return. She was a tall girl who wore her auburn hair in coronet braids. There was a peachy bloom on her cheeks; her Irish blue eyes looked both laughing and afraid. Tacy had been shy as a child and she was still diffident with teachers, some parents, most boys. But with Betsy and Tib she bubbled over with fun.

"I didn't laugh so much all the time I was in Milwaukee," said Tib, the day the three of them took a picnic up on the Big Hill.

They built a fire and made cocoa, smoky but delicious. Looking down the long slope, pied with goldenrod, asters and sumac, they told stories of their childhood, recalling how they had splashed themselves with mud and gone begging and how Tib had offered to marry the King of Spain. They planned triumphs for Tib in high school, paired her off hilariously with this boy and that one. Betsy repeated all the comments she had heard about Tib's coming.

"Heavens, Betsy!" cried Tib. "What have you been saying about me? I can never live up to it all."

"You can." Betsy was serenely sure.

"They'll be expecting a Billie Burke."

"You're prettier than Billie Burke."

"I admit I'm kind of cute," said Tib, prancing about. "I can fasten my father's collar around my waist."

"Tib! Not really!"

"Yes, I can. Of course," she added with characteristic honesty, "my father has a very thick neck. And I have a dark secret, a skeleton in my closet."

"What is it? What?"

"*Gott sei Dank,* skirts are long."

Betsy reached back to her Milwaukee visit for a shred of German. *"Was ist los? Was ist los?"*

"Erin go braugh!" shouted Tacy. "If you two are going to throw foreign phrases around, so will I. What is your dark secret?"

"Look!" Tib lifted her skirts dramatically, halfway to her knees. "I'm bowlegged! My dancing teacher broke the news to me. She doesn't think I can be another Adeline Genée."

"Do you mind awfully? About your dancing, I mean," Betsy asked.

"No. If I can't be a dancer, I'll be an actress."

Tacy was consoling.

"Well, the Deep Valley High School will never find out about your shame. Skirts are getting longer."

"And tighter," added Tib.

She began to tell them about the new styles, the long tight sleeves, the high directoire waistlines, the princesse dresses, the enormous hats. After the picnic they trooped down to her house and inspected her clothes.

She was very fond of purple in all shades. There were touches of purple, lavender and lilac on almost all the dresses which hung neatly on hangers in her closet, smelling of lavender water.

Tib now wore a pompadour like Betsy's. They tried

to tease Tacy into wearing one.

"No," said Tacy. "I want to go down in history as the only female of my generation who didn't wear a pompadour."

"But Tacy, you'll be a junior this year! An upper classman, just think!"

"I'll be an upper classman in coronet braids."

"Next Tuesday," said Tib, with a long expectant sigh, "is the first day of school."

On the first day of school, according to custom, Anna made muffins for breakfast. Betsy had a new sailor suit, navy trimmed with red and white, and Margaret had a brown one with brown and white checked ribbons. Nevertheless, it didn't seem like the first day of school.

In the first place, Julia wasn't going back. She didn't even get up for breakfast. By special permission from her father, who usually liked the family all present at meals, Julia celebrated her independence by sleeping through the breakfast gong.

And although Tacy came to call for Betsy and ate a muffin for luck, things still didn't seem natural, for Tib was with her, dancing along in a high-waisted lilac silk skirt and a thin white open-work waist.

Tib didn't flush easily as Betsy and Tacy did, but she was so excited today that color burned in her cheeks, making her look even prettier than usual.

"Meet my friend Tib Muller." "Meet my friend Tib

Muller," Betsy kept saying with elaborate carelessness along the crowded, clamorous highway which was High Street on the first day of school.

Tony sauntered up; Cab and Dennie came together, to give each other courage; Carney came, welcoming, with Irma, Alice and Winona.

In the Social Room the crowd around them was so deep that Betsy had no chance to look for Joe. She hadn't forgotten her plans, however. They were written in her mind as well as in her journal.

She caught a glimpse of Phyllis Brandish and waved. Phyllis waved negligently in return. Tib's triumph clouded Phyllis' arrival in high school and Betsy wondered whether Phyllis minded. But she didn't look envious.

The second bell, clanging loudly, drove them from the Social Room. They crowded through the upper hall past the case containing the cups for which the two societies, Philomathian and Zetamathian, competed annually: one for athletics, one for debating and one—as Betsy knew all too well—for essay writing.

They pushed on to the big assembly room with its alcove overlooking the rooftops of Deep Valley. Betsy, Tacy and Tib found seats together at the back of the junior rows. Miss Bangeter rapped for order and their junior year began.

4
Aft Agley

AFTER A HYMN, sung so lustily that it swam up to the ceiling and out the open windows into the treetops, Miss Bangeter read as usual from the Scriptures. The faculty sat on the platform, and Betsy observed that there were several new teachers. Some of the old ones were gone, and she was thankful that Miss Bangeter was not among the missing.

There was something noble about this high school principal. She was commandingly tall. A knot of black hair topped a dark hawk-like face which was usually grave, but knew how to flash into humor. Speaking with a Boston accent, she read rapidly but with intense conviction the parable of the sower and the seed.

After the Lord's Prayer, said in unison, the students made a quick round of their classrooms for registration.

Flanked by Tacy and Tib, Betsy went first to her English class. Foundations of English Literature, it was called this year. Mr. Gaston, a sardonic young man who had shepherded Betsy's class through composition and rhetoric, wasn't the teacher. He had been removed—rejoicing, it was said—to the science department. Betsy would have him for botany, she saw by a glance at her card.

She flourished the card toward Tacy.

"What do you think of this? They changed Gaston to science just in time to give him to us!"

"We're fated!" Tacy groaned. Mr. Gaston was an old enemy of Betsy's.

The new English teacher was named Gwendolyn Fowler. She had come from Miss Bangeter's Boston and looked not unlike her, having heavy black hair and white teeth. But she was short, shorter than

Betsy. Although young, she was completely poised and looked over the room with penetrating eyes, as though trying to pick out those pupils who would be hungry for what she had to give.

Joe Willard came into the room and Betsy's heart gyrated slightly. She poked Tib.

"There he is."

Tib whirled about to stare.

"No wonder you want to go with him! Who wouldn't?"

"Let's take him away from her, Tib," whispered Tacy.

"How can you? I haven't got him yet," Betsy whispered back.

But she would, she resolved.

He had grown over the summer, and he had changed. It wasn't only that he was better dressed—although he was. Last year he had been almost shabby. Today he wore a new brown suit and a brown striped shirt with a brown tie.

He seemed older; perhaps that was it. He had been traveling, of course, working with men. The summer in the harvest fields had hardened his muscles and had tanned him so deeply that his smooth pompadour and heavy eyebrows looked almost white. He had very blue eyes and a strong, well molded face. He walked with a slight, proud swing.

"He walks as though he knew he was somebody. Well, he is!" thought Betsy.

Although she liked English and was drawn to Miss Fowler, her attention wandered. She had resolved to speak to Joe and it agitated her, but she wouldn't let herself off. When the class was dismissed she strolled across the room.

She acted calm, like Julia, but her color deepened.

"Hello," she said.

His eyes warmed into friendliness. "Hello."

"How were the harvest fields?"

"Remunerative."

"Do you know that you've changed?" Julia had told her that it was good policy with boys to talk about the boys themselves. But that wasn't why she asked her question. It burst from her spontaneously.

"Sure," said Joe. "I've got calluses." He extended his palms.

Betsy spread out her own hands, glad that they were listed among her good points.

"Me, too," she said. "From rowing on Murmuring Lake."

"I don't see any. Softy!"

Betsy's color grew deeper still. She put her hands behind her.

"Isn't it a joke that we're having Gaston for botany? He's going to have his revenge about those apple blossoms." One of her quarrels with Mr. Gaston last year had pertained to the color of apple blossoms. Joe had taken her side.

"I'm sorry I won't be there to watch it. I'm taking physics."

"Grind!"

"Only softies take botany." He was laughing teasingly but all at once he stopped and said, "Well, I'll look for you when we start work on the Essay Contest."

"I probably shan't be chosen this year," Betsy replied plaintively. "There's a villainous Philomathian who always beats me. They'll put a better Zetamathian in. Anyway," she plunged boldly and smiled, "spring is a long way off."

He didn't rise to this bait; in fact he looked embarrassed, which for Joe Willard, famous for his poise, was most unusual.

"Oh, they'll give you another try at it," he answered lamely and looked so willing to terminate the conversation that Betsy said, "I hope so," smiled again and left him. He did not find a bantering parting word and this, too, was strange.

Betsy was puzzled at her failure.

"How did I look?" she whispered to Tacy as they moved on to the botany classroom.

"Cute," said Tacy.

Tib hooked her arm into Betsy's on the other side. "How did you come out?"

"Oh, I made a beginning."

Betsy wasn't, however, satisfied with this beginning, and she didn't know where the trouble lay. If he had acted bored she would have feared that he just didn't like her any more. But he hadn't acted bored, he had acted embarrassed.

"What the dickens?" she wondered, feeling depressed.

Mr. Gaston looked at her more kindly than of yore. He had a weakness for Julia. Passing mimeographed instructions for herbariums, he asked Betsy softly, "Has your sister left for the University?"

"Not yet," said Betsy. She tried to throw into her tone the implication that Julia couldn't bear to leave Deep Valley because it held Mr. Gaston.

He nodded gravely, and passed on.

Betsy and Tacy parted from Tib, who was taking German instead of Latin, and went into the Cicero class. There was another new teacher here, a young Swedish woman named Miss Erickson. Betsy didn't admire her, although she recognized that Miss Erickson was pretty, with a pompadour like the rising sun. Her light blue eyes were like marbles and her shirt waist suit was forbiddingly neat.

There was a peculiarity in her speech. She never

used a contraction. She said, "can not, do not, shall not," never, "can't, don't, shan't."

"She'll be hard," Tacy whispered to Betsy.

"She's probably a pill," Betsy said. Tib had brought the word "pill" from Milwaukee. It was the very newest slang.

It was good to pass from the chilly air of Miss Erickson's room to the warm, familiar quarters of Miss Clarke, who had taught them Ancient History and Modern History and this year would teach them the history of the United States. She was a gentle, trusting teacher. She and Betsy and Tacy were good friends, for she was Zetamathian faculty advisor and they were enthusiastic Zetamathians.

Last of all came Domestic Science. One great advantage to being a junior girl was that you were eligible to take Domestic Science. You went down the broad creaking stairs past the statue of Mercury, and the Domestic Science room was a fascinating place, provided with rows of little stoves, small shining pots and pans. They must each buy three white aprons, Miss Benbow said.

Miss Benbow wore an immaculate, stiffly starched white uniform, but her face, unlike Miss Erickson's, was not stiffly starched. It was a little worried, kind, and eager to please.

"I think I'm going to love Domestic Science," Betsy

said. "I hate housework at home, but it's different with other kids around."

"And we can eat up everything we cook!" Tacy replied.

"We'll give handouts to Tib."

Tib didn't take Domestic Science. Her mother thought it would be ridiculous, since Tib had known how to cook for many years.

They returned to the assembly room for dismissal and to the cloakroom to retrieve their hats. The noon whistles had not yet blown but school was over for the day. The first afternoon was traditionally spent by the Crowd buying books and going to the motion pictures, perhaps with a soda at Heinz's Restaurant afterwards. Betsy was expecting to follow this routine, but as the school filed out to the stirring strains of the march from *Aida* played by Carney on the piano she had a sudden thought.

Joe Willard had always worked at the creamery after school. But "after school" meant four o'clock. Since school ended at noon today, he might have the afternoon free.

She wouldn't seek him out. She had gone far enough already. But he might just possibly seek her out. He might regret having turned her off and want to make amends.

"I'll just make myself available," she thought, and

suggested casually, "Let's wait for Carney."

Tacy, Tib and Winona agreed.

They loitered at the wide limestone entrance. It was a warm day. Up and down High Street lawns were still green, gardens were still gaudy. It would have seemed like summer except for

> "... that nameless splendor everywhere
> That wild exhilaration in the air."

Betsy knew her Longfellow, but she only thought the lines. She didn't say them out loud.

Winona must have had the same feeling.

"Gee, it's a swell day!" she said. "We ought to go riding. Maybe Carney will take us all out in her auto."

"Why, there's an auto now!" Tib cried.

But it wasn't Carney's, and it wasn't Phil's. It was empty, although surrounded by an interested group.

Almost immediately, its owner came through the door. She was easily identified, for her hat was tied down by an automobile veil, in a smart bow under one ear. It was Phyllis Brandish, but for a moment Betsy hardly recognized her.

Phyllis, who was small, with olive skin and heavily fringed yellow-brown eyes like Phil's, usually had Phil's sullen expression. But she didn't look sullen now. Her face was lighted by a glowing smile as it turned up toward the face of the boy who accompanied her.

He, too, was smiling. And he was so taken up with the laughter between them that he didn't even see the group of girls. Poised, assured, Joe Willard touched Phyllis Brandish's arm as he walked with her out to the waiting automobile.

She climbed into the driver's seat. He cranked while she pulled down the throttle. And when that was done she moved over. He climbed in and took the wheel.

The roar and racket of an automobile in the throes of starting blasted against the ears of the waiting students. The fumes of gasoline poisoned the air. Then Joe and Phyllis, in Phyllis' machine, moved off down High Street, and the group of girls found their voices.

"Why, Betsy," Tib began, "I thought . . ." but Betsy nudged her.

"Joe Willard and Phyllis Brandish! That's a new one!" Winona said.

"It won't last long, I imagine," said Tacy, glancing at Betsy.

But Betsy remembered the glow on Phyllis' face, the smile in Joe's eyes. The reason Joe had seemed embarrassed after English class was because he already had a girl. He was going with Phyllis Brandish!

Betsy felt as though she had had the breath

knocked out of her. Maybe she could take him away from Phyllis if she tried, but she wasn't sure she wanted to. That look on Phyllis' face . . . ! And Phyllis had always seemed so bored and hateful. For all that she had traveled around the world, and had gone to exclusive schools, and had beautiful clothes, this was probably the most wonderful thing that had ever happened to her.

"Besides," thought Betsy, stiffening stubbornly, "if Joe Willard can afford to go with a girl and he wants it to be Phyllis Brandish, let it be Phyllis Brandish!"

The other girls were laughing and joking as they walked along High Street. Betsy was silent and she and Tacy dropped behind the others.

"What's that," she asked Tacy, "about plans ganging aft a-gley. Just where is a-gley? I'd like to know. It's where my plans have gone to."

She was joking but she felt hurt inside. She had always thought that when Joe Willard got around to girls, he would start going with her.

5
The Party for Phyllis

BETSY WAS PROUD BEFORE everyone in the world
except Tacy. She could hardly wait to persuade Tib
she didn't care at all that Joe Willard had driven off
with Phyllis Brandish.

"Really," she said, as soon as she and Tib had
parted from the others, with plans to meet on the Sibley lawn after dinner. "Really, I'm rather relieved. I

don't believe I want to settle down to one boy in my junior year. I think it would be a mistake."

Tib accepted this readily, as she accepted all Betsy's statements. She firmly believed that Betsy was the most wonderful creature in the world.

"Perhaps I'd better not start going with one boy, either," she answered anxiously. "What do you think, Betsy? Would it be a mistake for me, too?"

Betsy pondered. "Lloyd Harrington would like to go with you, I'm sure. And he's a great catch. I don't know, Tib. It just depends on what you want to do."

"I want to do whatever you do," Tib said. "If you don't want to go with just one boy, neither do I."

Betsy was glad to have her own attitude established before Irma's party for Phyllis, which took place on Friday afternoon. By Friday it was plain to the high school that Joe and Phyllis had a real case. She drove to school in her own auto as Phil did, in his. And every afternoon after classes she drove Joe down to the office of the *Deep Valley Sun*.

For it developed that Joe was no longer working at the creamery. After his return from the harvest fields he had been hired by Mr. Root, Winona's father, as a cub reporter and general handyman. Winona was bitter about it.

"I've been talking Joe Willard up to Papa for years," she said. "I told him Joe deserved something better than the job at the creamery. I told him Joe was the best writer in high school—excuse me, Betsy—and that he would make a swell reporter. And now he goes and gets himself a job on the paper and a girl, too."

"Take him away from her, Winona," teased Carney. "You have a wonderful chance. You can go down to your father's paper after school and hang around all you want to."

"That's a good idea," said Alice. "Especially since Pin has graduated." Pin had been Winona's beau last year.

"But there's Squirrelly, you know," said Winona, looking impish. "He kind of likes me, and I kind of like him."

Squirrelly was a senior with a headful of tight curls, high color and a deceptively bashful air. He was one of the stars of the football team. The supreme star was Al Larson, a brawny good-natured Dane who had been Carney's chief escort since Larry Humphreys and his brother, Herbert, had moved away to California. The Humphreys had gone with the Crowd in Betsy's freshman year. Larry and Carney had been really fond of each other. They still corresponded faithfully, a letter every week.

The day of Irma's party Betsy called for Carney. They joined Tacy and Tib at Lincoln Park and all walked together to Irma's house. It was a very warm day. They wore light summer dresses, held parasols, and all of them, except Betsy, carried little silk sewing bags on their wrists.

"Betsy," scolded Carney, "you ought to learn to sew."

"I despise sewing. I'm going to buy my dresses in Paris."

"But you ought to know how to embroider at least. There's so much sentiment in a gift you embroider. I embroidered Larry a laundry bag, and he was awfully pleased."

"Nobody would be glad to get anything I embroidered."

"I would," said Carney. "I'd love a hand-embroidered gift from you, Betsy."

"If I embroidered you a jabot, would you wear it?"

"Certainly I would."

"Is that a promise?"

"Certainly it's a promise."

"Girls, girls!" Betsy cried. "Be witnesses to this! If I embroider a jabot Carney promises to wear it. I'm going to call her bluff and embroider one."

"I'll help you," offered Tacy. "Me and my trusty needle."

"You'll help me! There's only one person in the world who would embroider a jabot worse than I would and that's you. You only carry that sewing bag because it matches your dress."

Tacy tried to hit her with it, but the ensuing chase was brief. Betsy stopped and patted her hair.

"We mustn't get hot and messy," she cried, "going to a party for the great Phyllis Brandish. My—almost—ex-sister-in-law."

Irma lived in a large substantial house, with porches and bay windows, set in a large lawn which had diamond-shaped flowerbeds on either side of the walk. Mrs. Biscay was soft-eyed and smiling like her daughter.

It was quite a large party because, since Phyllis was a senior, Irma had included a number of senior girls. Phyllis arrived late, wearing a dress of green Rajah silk cut in the new princesse effect and a large hat laden with plumes. She didn't try very hard to be friendly. She discussed Browner Seminary with Tib and seemed to take no interest in the things the girls told her about high school.

She didn't know whether she would be a Philomathian or a Zetamathian; she didn't expect to try out for the chorus; she smiled at the idea of going in for debating, and yawned when they discussed the football team.

"I doubt that I'll bother to go to the games," she said, "unless Joe has to cover them." She brought Joe into her conversation all the time. It was Joe this and Joe that.

"I think it's wonderful that Joe's a reporter," said Betsy.

"Is he doing just school news?" Alice asked.

"No," said Phyllis. "Lots of other things. He covers meetings in the evenings. It's a nuisance for me, but it's good experience for him. He wants to be a foreign correspondent, you know."

Betsy despised hearing Joe Willard's plans from Phyllis. She was the one he should have told about wanting to be a newspaper man!

"I think," she couldn't resist saying, "he's planning to go to college."

"Oh, of course," said Phyllis. "Naturally!"

But there was nothing natural, Betsy thought, about a boy without father or mother, who supported himself, going away to college. It was quite remarkable, in fact. She didn't say anything, however. She was careful to make sure that nothing in her manner gave a hint of her deep interest in Joe.

Irrationally, for she could take no credit, she felt proud of his new job. It was wonderful, she thought, for a sixteen-year-old boy to be even a part-time reporter. But it wasn't surprising that Joe had been able to do it. He had always been different from the general run of boys.

It was the reporter's job, of course, which made it possible for him to be friends with Phyllis. The Brandishes were rich. Their big rambling house across the slough was removed socially as well as physically from the rest of Deep Valley. Phyllis Brandish was snobbish. Betsy didn't think that Joe, wonderful as he was, would be acceptable to her if he were still working in the creamery.

As a reporter he was acceptable socially and he had always had an air. It wasn't only his striking blonde good looks; it was the way he carried himself. His life had made him more independent, more mature than the other boys. Compared to them he seemed like a man of the world. And the fact that he wasn't one of the high school crowd made him more desirable to Phyllis.

In a curious way Joe and Phyllis were alike. Neither one "belonged." They were different, Phyllis because she was rich and Joe because circumstances had always set him apart. He was accustomed to being different and had come to like it. Yes, Betsy thought, looking searchingly at Phyllis, who was chatting over an embroidery frame, in that way they were well matched.

"Always assuming," she thought, "that Joe brought plenty of money back from the harvest fields."

On second thought, she decided, he wouldn't need very much. He would need clothes, and he had evidently bought them. He was probably tired of dressing shabbily as he had been forced to do in his first two years of high school. As a reporter he would get passes to the shows that came to town, and since Phyllis had an auto and a big house to entertain in, he really wouldn't need more money than he earned.

Unconsciously Betsy kept watching Phyllis, trying to see something in the small-featured little face which could attract Joe Willard. To her Phyllis looked waspish, sharp, unlovable. But she conceded that the girl was pretty with her smooth olive skin and those strange eyes like her brother's, the great fluff of dark hair and her exquisite clothes.

"Probably," Betsy thought, "Joe doesn't realize how much those clothes do for her. He thinks that what they do for her is part of her. It almost is, for she has been rich all her life. She has an air, too."

She knew that Joe had not been influenced in his choice by the Brandish money or prestige. The fact that Phyllis was so cosmopolitan, that she had traveled abroad and had lived in New York—those things would fascinate him. But most of all, Betsy felt, their "differentness" drew them together.

She wondered how they had met and was glad when Carney asked the question.

"How did you and Joe get together, anyway?"

Phyllis laughed.

"I went to the *Sun* office to put in an ad for Grandmother; she was trying to find a new second maid. When I went back to my auto I couldn't get it started, and Joe came out and helped me."

"How did Joe Willard happen to know how to run a machine?"

"He learned this summer while he was working on a farm. The farmer had a Buick, too. Some farmers have a great deal of money, Joe says," Phyllis remarked, and seemed pleased to be able to offer information about such a strange species of human beings as farmers. Since almost all the girls had grandparents, uncles or aunts on farms they were both amused and plagued.

Irma's party was very elegant, with flowers all around the parlor and back parlor where the girls sewed and talked. At the dining room table there were more flowers, pink candles, little pink baskets filled with candy and nuts, even place cards. The refreshments were delicious—fruit salad, rolls, sherbet and two kinds of cake, devil's food cake with white frosting and angel food cake iced in pink. There were two dishes of sherbet apiece for those who wanted it, Irma announced. Most of the girls acclaimed this with enthusiasm, but Phyllis looked supercilious as she refused the second saucer.

"I simply can't like her," Betsy thought, and was relieved to observe that there was no real danger of Phyllis going with their Crowd. She thanked Irma graciously for their party but she didn't ask the girls to come to see her, and to Carney's impulsive, hospitable suggestion that she drop in on the Sibley lawn as most people did after school, Phyllis responded with a noncommittal smile.

After the party Betsy and Carney went down to the Lion Department Store and bought a jabot for Betsy to embroider. They were even more hilarious than usual in their reaction from Phyllis Brandish and from having acted so ladylike all afternoon. Carney asked Betsy to come home with her to supper and since they were still talking hard and fast at nine o'clock she invited her to stay all night. Permission was secured and Carney loaned a night gown.

Well-supplied with crackers, plums, layer cake, cheese and dill pickles, they looked over old snapshots and party programs, postal cards and souvenirs Larry had sent from California. They discussed the Humphreys.

Herbert and Betsy still corresponded too, but they weren't sentimental. They were what they had always called each other, "Confidential Friends."

Carney, in a sudden rush of words, grew confidential now.

"I wish I could see Larry," she said. "I'm afraid

that until I see him again, no one else is going to interest me."

She looked very serious, sitting in her long-sleeved night gown. Her hair, braided for the night, swung in neat pigtails.

"He'll come back to see you sometime," Betsy prophesied.

When Carney spoke again, she changed the subject.

"Do you know, Betsy, I was surprised when I heard that Joe Willard was going with Phyllis Brandish."

"Why?" Betsy asked.

"I always thought," said Carney bluntly, "that he would be a good one for you."

"Joe Willard?" Betsy asked. "Joe Willard?" She lay on her back and looked thoughtfully up at the ceiling. "He's a very nice boy. But to me he only means the Essay Contest."

Then it was Betsy's turn to change the subject.

"Doesn't it seem funny, Carney, to be a senior? Have you decided what you're going to do next year?"

"Yes," said Carney. "I'm going to go to Vassar if I can pass the exams."

6

Julia Leaves for the U

THE NEXT NIGHT BETSY and Julia hitched up Old Mag and went riding. It was almost unheard-of for Betsy not to be with a crowd of boys and girls on Saturday night. But for once she didn't want to be. Julia was leaving the following Tuesday.

Betsy had seen very little of her sister since returning

from Murmuring Lake. Miss Mix, the dressmaker, was in the house. Julia and Mrs. Ray were shopping all day long for materials and trimmings, as well as for hats, night gowns, underwear, shoes and all the other things Julia must take to the U.

"Anyone would think there wasn't a store in Minneapolis," Mr. Ray grumbled. "Why don't you just fill a trunk with her duds and let her buy what else she needs in the cities?"

But this was unthinkable. Mrs. Ray loved to shop. Every purchase must be discussed from all angles, colors matched, accessories pondered over. The two had been lost in a maze of clothes.

Betsy was glad tonight to have Julia to herself. It was a fine chance to talk, jogging along behind Old Mag, the reins held loosely, the whip in the right hand, but as a gesture merely. Old Mag always took her own gait.

Riding was a favorite evening diversion in Deep Valley, especially since Front Street and Broad Street had been paved. The Rays usually went as a family, Mr. and Mrs. Ray in the front seat, the three girls behind. They would drive down High Street past the high school and court house to the end, turn and drive up Broad past the library, the Catholic, Presbyterian, Baptist and Episcopal churches, and Carney's house. At Lincoln Park they would turn and angle down Second where there were more homes and more churches, livery stables, the post office, the fire house, the Opera House. Then, turning again, they would drive up Front past the Big Mill and the Melborn Hotel and Mr. Ray's shoe store. Sometimes they stopped for ice cream.

Out riding you continually passed and hailed friends who were likewise out riding, going up one street and down another while sunset died out of the sky. Occasionally an automobile whizzed past and then you had to hang on to the reins. Old Mag still detested automobiles.

Betsy held the reins tonight. Julia looked pensively over the pleasant streets, dimmed by the cool September twilight. She looked as though she were bidding them good-by, as indeed she was.

"I both hate it and love it," Julia said.

"Deep Valley? How could you possibly hate it?"

"Because it has held me for so long," Julia said. "And it isn't my native heath. Never was."

Julia was taking the music course at the U. She began talking about how hard she planned to work, not only at singing lessons but at piano, history and theory of music, languages.

"Of course," she explained, "the U wasn't my choice. What I would really like to do is go to New York or Berlin to study. But Papa thinks I'm too young for that, and I'm willing to go to the U first if he wants me to."

She drew her finely arched brows together.

"It's not so good, though," she said. "You ought to begin young in music. I'd like to start work with some great teacher. Geraldine Farrar made her debut when she wasn't much older than I am."

Betsy wanted to tell Julia how much she would miss her, but it didn't come easy to Betsy to say things like that.

"When you're gone, I'm going to go into your room every day and muss it up. I'm going to pull open your bureau drawers and throw your clothes on the floor. You know, make the place look natural."

"I'm not that bad, Bettina," Julia said, slipping her arm through her sister's.

"Worse! Gee, we're going to miss you!"

Old Mag's hoofs rang on the asphalt of Broad Street. Betsy and Julia bowed to the Brandishes, waved to the Roots, gazed thoughtfully at the first timid star.

"Yes, Papa and Mamma will miss me," said Julia at last.

"I'm going to stay around home more," Betsy said, awkwardly. "Go places with Mamma. Do the best I can."

"I'm very thankful that they have you, Bettina. I

don't see how 'only' children ever manage to leave home."

"Julia, I think I'll start taking piano lessons."

"What?" Julia received this declaration with such a cry of pleasure that it sent Old Mag into a trot. "Oh, Betsy, I'm so glad! How grand to have another musician in the family!" It was just like Julia to assume that Betsy's success at the instrument was already assured.

"I'll never be a musician," said Betsy. "But there has to be a piano being played around the Ray house."

"You'll study with Miss Cobb?"

"Of course."

Everyone in Deep Valley began piano study with Miss Cobb, a large, mild, blonde woman who was a Deep Valley institution, and one of its most widely admired heroines. Students of the piano who had any large talent ultimately went on to other teachers but their parents would have felt guilty about starting them with anybody but Miss Cobb. The fact that she had a particular gift with very small children was the least part of the explanation.

The town felt that Miss Cobb deserved its support. Years before, on the death of a sister, she had broken her own engagement to marry and had taken the sister's four children to raise. The little girl had followed her mother and the youngest boy had followed his sister. One of the two remaining boys was delicate. Miss Cobb kept on staunchly, year in and year out, teaching the young of Deep Valley to play.

"I remember," Julia said dreamily, "sitting down before the key-board and having Miss Cobb show me where middle C was. It's one of those memories that stand out like a photograph. There it is . . . me, aged six or so, all swelled up with importance, sitting on the piano stool with Miss Cobb's face quite close to me, and her gentle, kind voice saying, 'Now we always begin with middle C.'"

Julia stared at the star which was brighter now in the lofty leafy lane made by the treetops.

"If I were told today that I was beholding the Garden of Eden it couldn't possibly rate in importance with the way middle C seemed to me that day. It's queer, Bettina, to be thinking of that just as I'm leaving Deep Valley."

"Julia," said Betsy, "you talk as though you weren't ever coming back."

"I'm not," said Julia. She stared upward again and her violet gaze reached beyond the brightening star to wherever opera singers of the future were singing gloriously to hushed enraptured audiences. "Not to stay," she added. "Not in the way I'm here now."

Sunday morning Julia and Betsy went to the little

Episcopal church. They sang in the choir, and today, putting on their black robes and black four-cornered hats, both of them were aware that it might be a long time before Julia did it again.

The choir girls marched down the aisle, two abreast, singing. Julia looked rapt and far away, as always when she sang. But she loved the little brown stone church. Once during the prayers Betsy saw her lift her head and look around tenderly, then drop her face into her hands again.

Sunday night was always a special occasion at the Ray house. Friends of all members of the family dropped in for supper, which was called Sunday night lunch. Mr. Ray took charge, making the sandwiches for which he was renowned. There was talk and music. But tonight the shadow of Julia's departure hung over it all.

Everything was supposed to be just the same as usual, but it wasn't. Anna had baked a towering five-layer banana cake instead of the common uncomplicated kind. Mrs. Ray had provided roast chicken and other sandwich materials. Usually Mr. Ray made his sandwiches of anything which came handy— Bermuda onions, for example.

Most upsetting of all, Mrs. Ray had made a salad, a gelatin salad with fruit molded in.

"Why the salad?" Mr. Ray demanded, indignant.

"What's the matter with my sandwiches? Aren't they good enough?"

"Of course, darling!" Mrs. Ray cried. "Your sandwiches are marvelous. But I thought that just tonight, since Julia was going away . . ."

"What's that got to do with it? Anyone would think that Julia was going to the North Pole!"

But he felt as upset as anyone.

There was more company than usual, so many came to say good-by to Julia. Tony, unobtrusively helpful as always, passed sandwiches, poured coffee and made jokes with Mr. Ray about it being a wake.

"Bob Ray! You keep still! You stop that!" Mrs. Ray said.

When it was time for singing, Julia skipped the hymns and the old songs like "Annie Laurie" and "Juanita" . . . the kind which make people homesick. They sang "San Antonio" and "O'Reilly" and "Waiting at the Church" and that new song to which you danced the barn dance—

> "*Morning, Cy,*
> *Howdy, Cy,*
> *Gosh darn, Cyrus, but you're*
> *Looking spry. . . .*"

Everyone was noisier and gayer than usual, yet it wasn't a very successful Sunday night lunch.

The next day started off oddly: Julia was up so early. Her trunk was filled, closed and locked. It went off on the dray.

That night Mr. Ray took the family down to the Moorish Café. This was in the Melborn Hotel, which was run by the husband of Julia's singing teacher. Mr. and Mrs. Poppy, both stout, cosmopolitan and merry, joined the family at the table and it was a gayer occasion than the Sunday night lunch had been.

"New things are easier to do than old familiar things when there's going to be a change," Betsy decided profoundly.

It was hard for her to imagine what the house would be like without Julia, who had always been the buoyant center of it all.

On Tuesday, although Julia's train didn't leave until four forty-five, Betsy was excused from school at noon. Margaret had been excused, too, and Mr. Ray came home early from the store. These extravagant gestures were a mistake. The family sat around feeling strange, making conversation.

Mr. Ray asked Julia several times to let him know if her allowance wasn't big enough. He acted too cheerful. Mrs. Ray reminded Julia to buy some new jabots, and a pair of long kid gloves. Betsy made jokes that didn't come off and Margaret acted cross, which was always her defense against emotion. Anna kept coming in from the kitchen.

"Oh, my poor lovey! Going all the way to Minneapolis! Your bedroom will look like a tomb."

"No, it won't, Anna. I'm going to go in and muss it up, throw her clothes on the floor."

But the joke failed miserably.

"Her clothes have gone away already," Anna wailed. "The closet is as empty as though she had never been born. Charlie asked me last night, 'Did that McCloskey girl go away to the State University?' and I said, 'Na, Mr. and Mrs. McCloskey kept her right at home where she belonged.'"

At last, although Julia was going to eat supper on the diner, Mr. Ray went to the kitchen and put the coffee pot on. The Ray family always put the coffee pot on in moments of crisis. Anna brought out butternut cookies and everyone cheered up. They even got to laughing.

But just before she left for the train, when Old Mag was standing at the hitching post, Julia went to the piano and began to play. She played an operatic aria she had sung all last winter.

"*Mi chiamano Mimi. . . .*"

She sang a few bars and then broke off, and Mrs. Ray, waiting for her on the porch, wiped her eyes. And when Julia came out, very briskly, her eyes were red.

At the station things were exciting. School was over and Betsy's Crowd was there along with all of Julia's friends. Katie, rosy and smiling, had come down from the German Catholic College. Julia was a credit to Miss Mix in a new brown suit with a long fitted jacket cut in points, two in front and two in back. Her hat was enormous and she wore a corsage bouquet of little yellow roses.

Her face looked white and strained but she didn't cry again. Nobody cried. The Rays didn't believe in crying at trains. Margaret stood straight and smiled brightly at everyone who looked at her. When the train arrived the family trouped into the parlor car with Julia. Then they came out, and she appeared on the observation platform.

She smiled as the train pulled away and showed her white teeth set so close together. She leaned over the railing, blew kisses with both hands. She didn't look like Julia as Julia looked at home. She looked like Julia acting in a play.

Somehow that made everything easier. Mr. Ray took the family, Tacy, Tib and Katie up to Heinz's for ice cream. Everybody laughed and joked and felt better than they had felt for a week.

But when they got back to High Street the house seemed funny without Julia.

7

Howdy, Cy!

SCHOOL RUSHED IN TO try to fill the vacuum left by Julia's departure. School had a new flavor this year because of Tib. She was so small that when she sat at her desk in the assembly room her feet did not touch the floor. Miss Bangeter, to the general amusement, provided her with a footstool. Yet she made her presence felt. Half the boys in school were smitten with her, especially Lloyd and Dennie.

In September, as usual, the Zetamathians and Philomathians began a drive for members. Betsy was assigned to the membership committee and on Wednesday preceding the Monday on which the freshmen would choose their societies, the committee met in Miss Clarke's room.

Betsy went in with Carney, and was pleased to find Dave Hunt in the group.

"How that Dave Hunt has changed!" Carney whispered, and Betsy agreed. He had been in high school all along but he hadn't seemed important until this year. Over the summer he had been unaccountably transformed.

His extreme height—he was six foot three—was now impressive. Impressive, too, was his stoic calm. Dave Hunt seldom spoke but you knew it was because he did not wish to speak. He seldom smiled. But when a smile flickered over his stern, clean-cut face, it changed him from a deacon into a daredevil.

He was characteristically silent while Miss Clarke proposed brightly that money be appropriated to buy turquoise blue baby ribbon. The girls on the committee, Betsy and Carney, could make bows to pin on the new members. This was routine procedure.

"Maybe," suggested Betsy, "we might do something flashy this year. How about buying blue cambric and making arm bands for the Zets? Carney can sew."

"So can you," said Carney. "You're making me a jabot."

"Really?" asked Miss Clarke. "How nice! Sewing is such a valuable accomplishment."

Dave Hunt surprised everyone by speaking.

"Make a pennant, too," he said.

"A pennant?" "A big one?" Betsy and Carney waited radiantly.

Dave did not answer. His silence made it clear that when he said pennant he meant pennant, and that he couldn't possibly want a small one.

"Would we have any use for a pennant?" Miss Clarke asked, but her question was obviously rhetorical. "I don't suppose we'd be permitted to hang one on the stage unless the Philomathians did, too. Maybe it might work into the decorating, though. Certainly it would! That's a good idea, Dave," she added kindly.

Dave did not seem to hear her; she might have been a mouse squeaking. But the expression in his deep-set, dark blue eyes told Betsy and Carney that he expected a pennant. Two dollars were entrusted to the girls and they went down to purchase turquoise blue ribbon and cambric.

Thursday after school Carney hemmed arm bands while Betsy read aloud from "The Shuttle." They had saved a large piece of blue cambric and when the arm bands were finished they cut this into a triangle and Carney hemmed it.

"I hope it's big enough to suit him," Carney said. "He scares me. Doesn't he you?"

"He makes me feel about as big as a pin."

"Al says he's wonderful at football. He's sure to be a track star, too."

"He ought to be. Those long legs!"

Carney made her sewing very neat and Betsy inspected it with critically pursed lips.

Friday morning in the Social Room they approached Dave with an innocent looking package.

"Thanks," he said thrusting it into his pocket.

"Is it a secret what you're going to do with it?" Betsy asked, smiling.

But Dave didn't answer except with his calm gaze. That said, "Don't be silly. Of course it's a secret."

Monday morning Tacy and Tib called for Betsy as usual. Many Philomathians had been wooing Tib, but in vain. She already wore a blue rosette in her hair. Betsy and Tacy, of course, wore blue arm bands. These had been distributed to all Zetamathians secretly over the week-end. High Street was dotted with them, to the annoyance of passing Philos.

Cab, wearing an arm band, joined the girls. He was smiling broadly and several times, for no apparent reason, burst into a loud guffaw.

"Cab! What ails you?"

"You'll see."

Dennie, with arm band also, met them and the boys started ostentatiously to yawn.

"It's really too bad," said Tacy, "that you had to get up to go to school."

"We're going to school, but we didn't get up, did we, Dennie?"

"What do you mean?" asked Tib. "You must have gotten up. You went to bed."

"Oh, did we? That's what our mothers think."

"Well, you didn't stay up all night, did you?"

"All I've got to say," said Dennie, "is that it gets darned chilly along about three A.M."

This mystifying dialogue was interrupted by a cry from Tacy.

"Gee, is the school burning down? Look at that crowd!"

A churning mass of boys and girls extended from the big front doors out into the street. Cab and Dennie began to hurry and the girls kept pace. They saw that everyone was looking up at the cupola which rose high above the main building. They, too, stared up and saw something floating from the top of the peaked cap of roof. It was a turquoise blue pennant, the pennant Carney had hemmed.

Betsy, Tacy and Tib grabbed each other and began

to yell. After a moment Betsy paused to ask, "How did it get up there? That's a very steep roof."

"Search me," said Cab. "But it gets cold up in that cupola."

"Swell view of the sunrise, though," said Dennie, "and somebody had to stay on guard. . . ."

"Not that any Philo would dare—"

A Philomathian boy fell upon him from behind. As he thumped to the ground, Dennie grabbed the Philo. Boys were wrestling all over the school lawn. Dave Hunt, sober as always, was looking on and Betsy saw Joe Willard, grinning, take a swing at him. They locked in mock battle.

The gong, unusually loud and angry, broke through the uproar. Reluctantly holds were loosed, clothes straightened and boys and girls began to stream indoors. Everyone was talking at once.

"Who put it up?"

"He might have broken his neck."

"Squirrelly tried to get it down. He climbed as far as the cupola but Miss Bangeter stopped him. She's mad as a wet hen."

Carney pulled Betsy aside. "I feel like Barbara Fritchie or whoever it was made the flag."

"It was Betsy Ross, idiot." She lowered her voice and whispered, "Dave must have done it!"

Carney nodded. Her dimple pierced her cheek.

Miss Bangeter did indeed emit sparks of fury as she rapped the assembly to a semblance of order. She did not mention the pennant, however, and a noisy rendition of "The Men of Harlech" cleared the atmosphere somewhat. There wasn't much studying done that morning. A long ladder blocking the windows on the turret side of the building showed that the janitor was hauling down the pennant. But the query, "Who put it up?" still buzzed through classrooms and along the halls.

In the Social Room, after a tumultuous noon recess, the query was being answered. Nobody knew how the secret had slipped out. But it had.

"Dave Hunt put it up."

"Cab and Dennie and a bunch of other Zets stayed up in the cupola all night guarding it."

"Dave Hunt put it up."

"Dave Hunt."

"Dave Hunt."

Everyone was looking in Dave's direction, but his face was imperturbable.

When, at the end of the afternoon, the freshmen chose their societies, turquoise blue bows blossomed everywhere. The pennant, it was clear, had tipped the scales.

"You wait till next year. Just wait!" Philos were muttering. Winona hissed to the other girls after school, "Wait till next year. We'll get even."

Carney laughed. "Maybe you're going to get even now. Dave has been asked to stay and see Miss Bangeter."

"Gee, he's cute," said Winona forgivingly. "I wonder when he'll start taking out girls."

"He'll have to learn to talk first."

"Oh, I don't know. You could look at him."

No one ever heard what Miss Bangeter said to Dave, but no one had any doubt about what he said to her. Nothing, it was agreed. Nothing at all.

After the boiling excitement of this day the current of school ran smoothly. Junior class elections were held. Betsy was re-elected secretary. The junior girls were enchanted with Domestic Science. They began their study with canning, made grape jelly and peach jam. It was fun, as Tacy had thought it would be, to eat what they cooked.

Next to Domestic Science, Betsy liked Foundations of English Literature under little Miss Fowler. United States History as Miss Clarke taught it was supremely restful. In Cicero they struggled through the First Oration against Cataline under Miss Erickson's hard, marble-blue eyes.

They were supposed to be making herbariums for botany but not Betsy nor Tacy nor Tib had yet begun. The fall flowers were still abundant. It seemed such an easy thing to do to pick and press just one of each kind, that they forgot to do it.

Yet September was passing. Chauncey Olcott, as much a part of the season as the goldenrod, came to the Opera House. *Ragged Robin*, said the Rays, who went in a body as usual, was the best play he had had in years. It teemed with "good little people," banshees, will-o'-the-wisps, and tenderly wistful songs.

"Don't You Love the Eyes that Come from Ireland?"—Betsy thought of Tacy when she heard that one. "Sweet Girl of My Dreams" was almost as appealing as "My Wild Irish Rose," which Chauncey Olcott, wearing a plumed hat, sang as always after the second act.

Tony brought the songs up to the Ray house next day, but there was no one to play them! Betsy, who always found it easier to make plans than to carry them out, had not yet started her piano lessons. Not that she didn't miss Julia's music. It was unbelievably strange to have the piano silent. Mrs. Ray knew how to play but she had stopped practising since Julia had become so proficient. She never touched the instrument now except when Betsy had company and asked for her famous waltz and two-step. Fortunately, Carney could play and so could Winona. So the Crowd still sang sometimes around the Ray piano.

But having Tony bring the Olcott songs reminded

Betsy sharply of her resolution. At supper that night she said, "I believe I'll start taking piano lessons, if you still want me to."

"We certainly do," her mother said. And Mr. Ray added, "I could stand a few scales myself."

Betsy telephoned Miss Cobb and the next Saturday morning she walked down to Miss Cobb's house on a steep hillside street below the high school.

Betsy knew the little house from the days when Julia had studied there. The rooms were small, low-ceilinged, always comfortably warm and smelling of the potted geraniums Miss Cobb kept in the windows. There were a grand piano and an upright piano in the front parlor. In the back parlor was Leonard, the nephew who was ill. A slender fifteen-year-old boy with sandy hair and vivid cheeks, he often lay on a couch listening to the music. Bobby, the younger boy, was like his aunt, large and robust.

Miss Cobb's red-gold hair was dimmer than it had been when Julia studied with her. She wore glasses on a chain and snowy shirt waists belted neatly above black flowing skirts. Miss Cobb gave a feeling of largeness, and not only because of her Junoesque figure. It was the expression in her face, calm and courageous.

She was a gentle teacher. Under her tutelage you didn't have to worry too much about practising scales. Soon you were playing "The Merry Farmer" and "The Sailor Boy's Dream." She herself had studied abroad under a very fine master.

"She's a better musician than she is a teacher," Julia had remarked one time.

"And a finer human being than either," Mr. Ray had added.

Miss Cobb whirled the piano stool now until it was the proper height and Betsy sat down. Miss Cobb struck a note and said, as she had said to Julia, "This is middle C." Betsy liked that. It gave her a warm feeling of the continuity of life. Though she knew that she could never learn to play the piano as Julia did, she was glad she had begun.

Betsy missed Julia. Close as she was to Tacy, wonderful as it was to have Tib back, she missed the confidential talks in her sister's once brightly cluttered room. Now the room looked so unnaturally neat that she could not bear to go inside it.

The whole family missed Julia. Anna kept forgetting and would set five places at the table.

"That's a sign Julia wishes she was home, the poor lovey," Anna said darkly.

Mrs. Ray would never leave the house until the mail came and when there was a letter she telephoned Mr. Ray. They read them over and over and Betsy often read them aloud in the evening, Margaret sitting on her father's knee.

They were good letters. Just as Julia had always shared everything—bon bons, handkerchiefs, her excitement over a new opera or book—she was trying lovingly now to share this new experience. She described the campus, her classrooms and teachers, the dormitory where she lived. Roger had taken her to lunch in Minneapolis. She had found a bewildering number of friends.

She sounded happy. Nevertheless, there was that in her letters which told that Anna's divination might be correct. The pages were so full of longing and remembering. She asked about everything and everyone at home. The family wrote to her often. Betsy weighed the postman down with fat and supposedly funny letters. Yet Julia kept asking for more and more.

One evening toward the end of September Betsy wrote a long letter to Julia. She finished her homework and her telephone conversations, wound her hair on Magic Wavers and went to bed. Margaret was already asleep and Anna had gone up to her lofty room. Mr. Ray wound the clock and Mrs. Ray put Washington and Lincoln in the basement. Nobody locked doors in Deep Valley. Soon the lights were out and the house was still.

Betsy had barely fallen asleep when she was awakened by the sound of music. The air was shattered by great crashing chords. It was the new song everyone was barn-dancing to.

> *"Morning Cy,*
> *Howdy Cy,*
> *Gosh darn, Cyrus, but you're*
> *Looking spry. . . ."*

Betsy started up, but her room was dark. She ran to the door. The whole house was dark. In the upper hall she bumped into her mother and father. Mr. Ray was striking matches. From downstairs the music continued jubilantly.

> *"Right in line,*
> *All the time,*
> *Jiminy crickets, but you're*
> *Looking fine . . ."*

Nobody could play like that but Julia.

Betsy, Wavers and all, rushed down stairs, followed by Margaret, rubbing her eyes, and her mother, in a nightdress, and Anna, who came down from the third floor holding a lighted candle and shouting "Stars in the sky!" Just as they reached the landing Mr. Ray succeeded in lighting the gas.

Julia sat at the piano, playing, with tears streaming down her face.

"Julia!" The music broke off. Everyone fell upon her with hugs and kisses.

"What's the matter?" asked Mr. Ray. "Get fired?"

"No," said Julia. "I just got homesick and so I came home. Mr. Thumbler brought me up in the hack."

She wept and everybody wept.

"I never knew, until I went away from home, how nice we all are!" Julia sobbed.

"Oh, we are, are we?" asked Mr. Ray. He went up stairs and put a bathrobe over his nightshirt. When he came back he said, "Well, I'll go put the coffee pot on."

"Bring it up to our room," said Mrs. Ray. "We'll all get in bed there."

Betsy and Margaret went upstairs and piled into bed beside their mother. Julia sat down joyfully, taking off her hat and coat. She was going to stay until Sunday night, she said, pulling pins out of her hair. She hadn't needed to ask permission to come. At the U you were allowed a certain number of cuts.

"I just don't want to use all of mine in case I get homesick again."

Mr. Ray came up, a broad smile on his face, bearing a tray with a pot of steaming coffee, cream, sugar and cups. Anna brought cookies, apples, cold pie, a glass of milk for Margaret.

"Stars in the sky!" she kept saying, shaking her head. "Wait 'til I tell Charlie."

She went to bed then, but the rest stayed awake a long time, listening while Julia told about life at the University.

8

Those Things Called Sororities

JULIA HAD EXTRAORDINARY things to tell. Immediately upon her arrival at the University various strange girls had begun to deluge her with attentions. They had sent her flowers. They had offered to show her around the campus, to help her register, and to guide her to her classrooms. "Why, how kind of them!" Mrs. Ray cried. She sat upright in bed, the tray on her knees, looking at Julia with alert blue eyes. Her curly red hair fell around her shoulders over her lace-trimmed white night gown.

Betsy and Margaret wore outing flannel night gowns. Betsy, bristling with Magic Wavers, and Margaret, with little braids bereft of ribbons sticking out on either side of her small solemn face, leaned against their mother's shoulders, right and left.

Betsy cradled a cup of well-creamed and sugared coffee. She liked the warmth of the cup and the coziness of being three in bed; for the room was cool, although Mr. Ray had closed the window and opened the drafts in the furnace. Julia was wrapped in her mother's bathrobe. Mr. Ray, beaming with pleasure, sat cross-legged in the other easy chair.

"I didn't realize," he said, "that our State University was such a friendly place."

"It isn't," Julia answered. "I thought it was at first. Then it dawned on me that not all the new girls were being treated the way I was. Just a few of us were getting all this attention."

"I'm not surprised that you were one of them," Mrs. Ray put in. The members of the Ray family never made a secret of their admiration for each other.

"But how did it happen? What was up?" asked Mr. Ray.

"Those girls," Julia continued, her deep tone emphasizing the gravity of her words, "belonged to sororities. They were rushing me—that's the word they use. They want me to join, but I can't do it yet. Freshmen aren't allowed to join sororities—they can't even be asked—until spring."

"What is a sorority?"

"The word means 'sisterhood.' Isn't that nice, Bettina? And men have fraternities, 'brotherhoods.' Fraternities and sororities are terribly important. They are absolutely the most important things on the campus."

"Does everybody belong to one?" asked Mr. Ray.

"Oh, no. Just a fraction of the students."

"I don't see how they can be so important then." Mr. Ray selected an apple and started to peel it neatly with a little pearl-handled penknife.

"Each sorority has its own house," Julia went on eagerly, shaking back her loose dark hair. "The girls who belong to a sorority live in their house instead of in the dormitory. They have a chaperone and a cook and other servants. They give marvelous parties and invite the fraternity men. And the fraternity men give marvelous parties and invite the sorority girls."

"How do the people who don't belong manage to have some fun?" asked Mr. Ray, taking care that the peeling did not break.

"I have no idea," said Julia. "You simply have to belong to a fraternity or sorority if you want to have any fun."

"Seems kind of tough on those who don't." Mr. Ray laid the peeling carefully in an ash tray and quartered his apple, removing the seeds. He gave a quarter to Margaret who had been watching him expectantly, and he offered one to Betsy, but she shook her head. She was listening in rapt fascination.

"Have you been inside one of those houses?" she demanded.

"Yes," answered Julia. "To teas at the Epsilon Iota house, and the Alpha Beta house and the Pi Pi Gamma house. They aren't allowed to entertain freshman at anything but teas until spring. In April there's a week of rushing. Dinners, luncheons, parties of all kinds are crowded in. Girls who are being rushed by two or three sororities have a simply frantic time."

"I trust it doesn't come at examination week," said Mr. Ray. But nobody listened to him.

"What did they do at the teas?" Betsy wanted to know.

"Oh, the food was yummy! The tables were decorated with the sorority colors and the girls stood around the piano and sang their sorority songs. They wear pins and have a grip and a password. Of course, you don't find out what the grip and the password are until you are initiated."

"Sounds like a lodge," said Mr. Ray. "But lodges are open to anyone. It must be the same with those sorority things. It has to be. The University is supported by the taxpayers' money. Any boy or girl ought to be allowed to join—"

"Oh, but they aren't!" cried Julia. "The sororities are very, very exclusive. I'm lucky, I can tell you, that three of them are rushing me."

"Have you any idea which one you want to join?" her mother asked.

"Yes. I knew right away. The Epsilon Iotas. They're just my kind. I'm going to be an Epsilon Iota. And if I am, Bettina, you will be too, and so will Margaret. Sisters always join their sister's sorority."

"Gee!" Betsy cried. "I'd love to be an Epsilon Iota." The tray made bouncing impractical, but she reached behind her mother's back to tweak one of Margaret's braids. "How about being an Epsilon Iota, Margaret?"

"I'm a Baptist," said Margaret, blinking rapidly to prove that she was wide-awake. Everybody laughed.

"Well, I'd like to find out a little more about these sororities before you join one," Mrs. Ray said. "I'll go down to the library tomorrow and look them up. What I can't make out is how they knew they wanted to rush you. Did they pick you out just because you were attractive?"

"Oh, someone must have recommended me. Someone here in Deep Valley. Perhaps one of the teachers."

"What about that little Parrott girl who went up to the University last year?" asked Mr. Ray.

"She's a barb."

"What's that?"

"It stands for barbarian. It's what they call all non-fraternity and non-sorority people. It's sort of a joke, of course."

"Not a very funny one," said Mr. Ray. "The little Parrott girl is a very fine girl. I've sold her shoes all her life. She waits and buys them from me now when she's home for vacation instead of buying them in the Twin Cities."

Julia jumped up and hugged him, laughing. "She may buy her shoes from you but she isn't a sorority girl. Probably she doesn't want to be. I've seen her around the campus. She's awfully wrapped up in her studies."

"After all, that's what she's there for," grumbled Mr. Ray. He, too, got up and took the tray from Mrs. Ray's knees. "You all hustle off to bed now. Margaret's asleep already."

"No, I'm not." Margaret opened her eyes wide but she closed them again when her father picked her up and carried her away.

"I'm not sleepy at all," said Betsy. She was enthralled with Julia's romantic sisterhoods.

"Don't you go into Julia's room and talk," Mrs. Ray warned. "It's cold and you both need your sleep. Besides, I don't want to miss anything."

"She hasn't begun on Roger yet."

"We'll save him till morning," Julia said. "I'll unpack my dream robe and get right in bed."

"Your dream robe?" asked Betsy. "What's that?"

"It's what we call night gowns up at the U," Julia said. She kissed everybody and went into her room, tossing her shoes ahead of her and flinging her clothes on a chair. She was singing as she went:

> *"Howdy Cy,*
> *Morning Cy,*
> *Gosh darn, Cyrus, but I'm*
> *Feeling spry. . . ."*

"Gee," cried Betsy. "It's grand to have you home!"

True to her word Mrs. Ray went to the library next day. It was hard to tear herself away from Julia but she did. Julia visited school, looking very citified in her brown suit and hat. She went to see Miss O'Rourke, who had always been her favorite teacher and Miss Clarke, whom she called "dear old Clarke!" and Miss Bangeter, who was like everybody's conscience. Julia had dropped the student-teacher attitude. She treated the teachers as though they were her age or she theirs. She actually joked with them.

"I wonder whether I'll be like that my first year out of high school," Betsy thought.

After school the house was crowded. The Kellys dropped in, and Tib and Tony and a host of Julia's friends. At supper Mrs. Ray told the family about her research.

"I explained to Miss Sparrow that Julia was going

to join a sorority," she said, "and that I wanted to make sure she joined a good one. Miss Sparrow brought out the encyclopedia and the University catalogue and some other books, and I copied down the dates and places where the different sororities were founded. But I couldn't find out what the names meant."

"They're Greek letters, of course."

"I know, and they all stand for something, but the books don't say what. Do you know, Julia? It would help to get a line on them if we knew what their names meant. It would show us their ideals—"

"Mamma," said Julia, "you don't need to bother looking up anything more about sororities. I know which one I want to join. I want to join the Epsilon Iotas. I don't give a hoot what the name means. The girls just suit me. My idea of heaven is to be an Epsilon Iota and live at the Epsilon Iota house."

"Well," said Mr. Ray, "That settles that!"

Julia's visit was almost swallowed up by talk of sororities. There was a stream of company, of course; there were Julia's favorite things to eat; and there was music. Sisterhoods or no, Julia must show her mother and Betsy how her voice had improved, how the high tones were coming out and about the new idea in breath control. Her teacher was German, Fraulein Hertha von Blatz. She was very fine, Mrs. Poppy said. Julia talked about Roger, too, and other college men. She never said "college boys" any more; it was always "college men."

But they talked sororities at every spare moment, especially when Tacy and Tib were around. Julia was given to enthusiasms and she knew how to communicate them. The Epsilon Iota house became in her description an enchanted domicile. The various Epsilon Iotas—the dark, queenly one, the red-headed one, the twins, the stunning blonde—moved through Betsy's head like characters in a romance.

In Julia's window seat at night, Betsy plied her sister with questions. She learned that a sorority had a ritual which members went through at every meeting. She learned that initiations were mystical secret affairs. Secrecy, in fact, was the core of the fruit. The girls were bound together by secret vows.

"How can they be sure they like each other?"

"No girl can get in unless everyone wants her. There has to be a unanimous vote," Julia explained.

"But don't they ever have fights?"

"Probably not. It's all on a pretty high plane."

Sunday evening Julia went back to the University, and Betsy slept that night with sororities rolling about in her head like billiard balls.

She woke early, suddenly, as she often did when she had great ideas. The sky was stained dark red and gold, as though the trees on Deep Valley's circling hills had pushed their autumn colors up into the sky, but all were dull yet, unburnished by the sun.

Why not start a sorority, Betsy thought? She and Tacy and Tib. They had been friends so long. What could be more fitting than that they should be founders of a sorority?

A sorority was just what she needed to fill her winter. That had seemed empty somehow, since Joe Willard upset her plans by starting to go with Phyllis. She did not admit it often, but she felt hollow inside whenever she thought of that. None of her resolutions seemed important any more, except for the piano study, which gave her a healthy satisfaction. Her morale needed bolstering, and a sorority was so new, so dramatic.

"Of course," she thought, a smile playing around her lips as she lay in bed looking at the sunrise, "we couldn't have ours quite so serious as the real ones. Winona would never take any highfalutin' vows, and Irma and Tib are such gigglers. But we could have pins. We could have grips and passwords and a ritual—I could write it myself."

She jumped out of bed smiling, and going to the bathroom she took the cold bath she reserved for moments of decision. She took her curls down, with even more care than usual, and put on her most becoming dress.

At school she wrote notes to Tacy and Tib.

"I have something terribly secret and important to talk over. Can't we shake the others after school?"

9
Okto Delta

ON A GOLDEN HILLTOP overlooking Deep Valley,
Betsy, Tacy and Tib founded their sorority. They sat
in a grove of small maples, all the same color and
ridiculously bright. Below them autumn flowed like
spilled wine. Not only the trees, but the bushes, the
vines, even the grasses were ruddy. Descending rows
of rooftops glittered in the sun.

The girls had escaped from the Crowd by a series of manoeuvres. They left school by a side door, walked to the street below High Street, walked along that for two blocks, and entered the Ray house at the back. Anna was up in her room, and they foraged for food with muffled laughter which brought Margaret into the kitchen.

"We're going for a ride," Betsy explained. "A very mysterious, important ride."

A sympathetic smile quivered across Margaret's little face.

"Can I go, too? I'm all alone. Mamma's gone out."

"I'm sorry," Betsy said, "but this is something secret, Margaret." She felt a little wrench of guilt as Margaret's smile died away. "Will you help us, dear? We don't want anyone to know where we are, so if the doorbell rings don't answer until we're gone."

"All right," Margaret agreed. She went slowly back to the parlor, with her erect, dignified tread.

The girls found grapes and crackers. The front doorbell started to ring and they slipped out the back door. They dashed across lots to the barn, hitched up Old Mag and climbed into the surrey.

"Let's go up Agency Hill," Tacy suggested. "There's such a beautiful view."

This steep road had led to an Indian Agency back in pioneer days. Tom's Grandmother Slade told stories about it. Old Mag dragged the surrey patiently to the summit, where the girls turned off on a shoulder of the hill. At the maple grove they loosened Old Mag's checkrein and left her under a pink-gold tree.

"Now, what's it all about?" asked Tib, throwing off her hat. Tacy tossed off her hat, too. The yellow head and the auburn one looked like bright leaves drifting down as the girls sank to the ground.

Betsy added her hat to the pile. But she didn't sit down. Hazel eyes glowing, she swayed on her toes.

"Let's us—the three of us—start a sorority."

Tacy and Tib were stunned for a moment by the magnificence of the concept.

"Do you mean a real one?" Tacy asked.

"Just like they have at the U. Greek letters and all."

"What would they stand for, the letters?"

"Gosh, I don't know! We'd have to make something up." Betsy sat down in front of them, looking earnestly into their faces. "We're good ones to start a sorority. You know what the word means—sisterhood—and we've been friends so long. A thing like this would hold us together always."

"We'd hold together anyway, I imagine," said Tib. "We held together all the time I was in Milwaukee."

"But Tib! If we made vows of friendship. . . ."

"We don't really need any."

"Well, it certainly couldn't hurt to make them," replied Tacy. "I can't think of anyone I'd feel safer about promising to like." This struck her so funny that she burst out laughing. "Wilt thou, Betsy Ray, take me, Tacy Kelly, in holy bonds of friendship?"

"I wilt," chanted Betsy.

"Me, too!" shouted Tib, and began to fling leaves with such vigor that presently Tacy was gasping in the grass and Betsy's hair had fallen down.

She twisted it up determinedly.

"Stop acting like five-year-olds! Seriously, isn't it a grand idea?"

"It's a marvelous idea."

"It's a swell idea. Especially," added Tib, reaching for a grape, "if we give lots of parties."

"Oh, yes, we'll give parties and invite the fraternity men."

"What fraternity men?"

"Why, the boys." Betsy opened the box of crackers and they all began to munch. "We three will write the constitution and the ritual. And then we'll send invitations to the girls and ask them to join, and we'll have a meeting and initiate them."

"Who shall we ask?"

"Just the Crowd. Sororities are terribly exclusive. Let's see, there are three of us. Carney, Alice, Winona and Irma make seven. It would be nice to have eight, to make two tables of cards."

"Katie is pretty lonesome now that Julia's gone away. If you don't think she's too old . . ." Tacy hesitated.

"I'd love to have Katie. She's such a good sport."

"And we wouldn't always have to have a chaperone if she was along," Tib pointed out.

"That's right. Now we have to think of a name."

Betsy stretched out on her back. Tib sat with her face in her hands. Tacy dropped her head into crossed arms. There was silence in the grove, except for the rustling made by an exploring squirrel.

"These aren't oak trees, if you're looking for nuts," Betsy murmured. "Go away and let us concentrate."

She sat up suddenly.

"Do you think the name ought to be serious? We three feel serious about it, of course. But you know Winona. We'll have to make it sort of devilish to appeal to her."

"How about Eight Devils?" Tib inquired.

Betsy and Tacy stared in admiring unbelief.

"Eight Devils!" "Why, that's perfect!" "Tib Muller, I didn't think you had it in you!"

Surprised but elated at this triumph, Tib preened herself. "I think it's pretty good, too."

"Eight Devils!" Betsy repeated. "Now we have to put it into Greek. Who do we know who speaks Greek?"

"Probably Miss Erickson does, but I wouldn't ask her, the old pill!"

"Miss Bangeter knows everything, but she might not . . . she might not . . ." Betsy didn't finish the sentence. The others understood.

"Miss Sparrow would know." Miss Sparrow was Deep Valley's popular librarian.

"Of course. We'll ask Miss Sparrow. It's only the word eight we need to bother about. Devil begins with D and I know the Greek letter. It's shaped like a triangle. It's Delta."

"We're the Eight Deltas," shouted Tib. She jumped to her feet and started shwushing through the leaves. "I'll make the invitations, Betsy. I'll draw horns in all the corners and maybe a devil's pitchfork."

"Swell. We'll make them tomorrow after school."

"When will we write the constitution and stuff?"

"The day after that." Betsy rocked with joy. "Let's have the initiation Saturday night. We can have it at my house."

"Let's have a mock initiation before the real one. Put ice down their backs—that sort of thing."

"Oh, let's!"

"I feel as though we were kids again, making up a club," said Tib.

Betsy turned on her indignantly. "This isn't any kiddish club, Tib Muller! It's a sorority. You're going to take a vow never to get mad at us."

"I never get mad at you anyway."

"She's hopeless," Betsy said to Tacy. "Let's go ask Miss Sparrow."

They went back to Old Mag, who whinnied a

welcome. Betsy fixed the checkrein, and they climbed into the surrey. They drove down Agency Hill to the library, talking all the way about pins, grips, passwords, whistles and salutes. With windblown hair and pink cheeks they burst in on Miss Sparrow.

"Miss Sparrow, what's the Greek word for eight?"

"Eight? Let me see! Why, it's o k t Ω," she replied.

"How do you spell it?"

"O-K-T-O."

"That's all!"

"Thank you!"

They rushed back outside. "We're the Okto Deltas!" "The Okto Deltas!"

"It sounds wonderful!" Betsy exclaimed, blissfully uncritical of the fact that it was a hybrid name, that Okto was a Greek word while Delta was only the Greek initial of an English word. It sounded just as good as Epsilon Iota.

Next day, all three were wool-gathering in classes. They deluged one another with notes and dodged their mystified friends. After school they went downtown and purchased cardboard, orange and black crayons, orange and black crepe paper. Orange and black, they had decided, were to be the Okto Delta colors.

They went to Tib's house, and locked in her room, they made the invitations. Tib cut the cardboard into diamond shaped pieces, which she folded into double

triangles. The outer flap was colored orange and outlined in black to make a Delta. Superimposed was the
black letter O with a devil curled inside. On the inner
flap, the recipient was invited to come to Betsy's
house on Saturday night to join the mystic order of
Okto Delta.

Tib mailed the invitations next morning on her
way to school, and when the three girls gathered that
afternoon at Tacy's house, Katie's invitation, post-
marked and looking very official, lay on the hall table.

They locked themselves in Tacy's room and began
the constitution, Tib writing, Betsy dictating, Tacy
adding witty bits. Before they had finished, the telephone began to ring. The other girls had come from
school and found their invitations.

Excitement seethed over the wire and through the
Crowd next day. When the boys found every girl
engaged for Saturday night, they were curious and
annoyed.

On Saturday it started to rain, a steady downpour.

"It's perfect, just perfect for an initiation," Betsy
rejoiced.

Tacy and Tib came for supper, and after supper, in
spite of the rain, Mr. and Mrs. Ray obligingly went to
the Majestic, taking Margaret with them.

The first thing the girls did was lock all the doors
and pull the shades. They tacked blankets over the
parlor windows. There were orange and black candles

in readiness but they didn't light them. Instead, when they had finished their work, they extinguished all lights everywhere.

The initiates found a dead black house veiled with sheets of rain. Early arrivals were forced to stand on the porch until all five had come. When the door was opened, Irma entered first.

"Shake the hand of friendship," said a deep sepulchral voice. Irma clasped a shadowy hand. Then her terrified scream rang out. Carney followed and she screamed. So did Alice. Winona and Katie were made of sterner stuff. Katie grasped the hand without a word, and Winona cried scornfully, "Calm yourselves, children! It's just a glove filled with cracked ice."

In the jet black parlor they were told to kneel in a circle. Again each girl screamed in turn as a small piece of ice slithered down her back. They were told by the sepulchral voice, sounding now more like Tacy's, and shaky with laughter, that they must eat worms.

"Sure. I like worms," said Winona. "Can I have a second helping? It's spaghetti, kids."

"It isn't! It's worms! It's horrible!"

The pandemonium became so great that it seemed best to light the candles. The founders were revealed dressed in sheets trimmed with black and orange crepe paper.

"Now sit down in a row. Make quick!" commanded Tib.

Betsy unfolded a sheet of foolscap paper and began to read.

"Respectfully submitted, the Constitution of the Okto Delta sorority. . . ." A sorority, she paused to explain, was a sisterhood. They were banding themselves together into a sisterhood.

"Hi, Sister Biscay," Winona hailed Irma.

"Howdy, Sister Root," cried Katie.

Tib rushed to silence them and Betsy continued:

"'Okto,' be it understood, is a Greek word meaning eight. 'Delta' is the Greek equivalent of the English letter D, which in this case stands for Devils, leaving the translated name of the sorority—"

"Eight Devils!" Winona interrupted. "Whoopee!"

Betsy frowned severely.

"The purpose of the sorority," she went on, "is to have a good time. The only theory it has to expound is, 'Laugh and the world laughs with you.' Requirements are being jolly, sticking by the bunch, and treating everybody square."

She proceeded to the rules and by-laws.

The officers, elected by ballot once a year, would be president, secretary-treasurer and sergeant-at-arms. The initiation fee would be two cents, the monthly dues ten cents. Money thus accumulated was to be used at the discretion of a social committee.

This committee, composed of two girls, would make arrangements for at least one festivity every two weeks.

"For example," Betsy interjected, "dances, picnics, cross-country tramps, mock weddings and stag parties."

Each member was to entertain the sorority every eighth Saturday evening in alphabetical order. Refreshments would be served.

"And they'd better be good!" someone shouted.

"We must now take the sacred vow of friendship," Betsy said, and Tib went around with an ink pot and a pen and everyone was asked to sign.

Winona took the pen doubtfully. "Do you mean that I have to stay friends with all of you forever?"

"That's right," Betsy replied.

"What if Irma takes Squirrelly away from me?"

"She can't. She's your sister in Okto Delta. She has to leave all our beaux alone."

"Heck!" said Winona, signing. "That alone is worth the dues."

Irma threw a sofa cushion.

"Sister Biscay! Sister Root!" cried Tib, dashing about.

Order was restored and elections were held.

Carney was elected president.

"I don't mind mentioning to the Sistren," Betsy said, "that I expect to be secretary-treasurer. I want the fun of writing up the minutes. I've even bought a notebook. See?"

"And I don't mind mentioning," said Tib, "that I expect to be sergeant-at-arms. You notice how well I've been keeping order. I'm little, but oh my!"

Obligingly, the Sistren made Betsy secretary-treasurer and Tib sergeant-at-arms. Betsy whipped out a pencil and began to write the minutes, reading them aloud when she thought they were exceptionally brilliant.

"The first thing to do," said Carney, taking charge, "is to decide on a whistle. We simply have to have a whistle. Otherwise how would we know whether it was an Okto Delta trying to call us away from our supper or just some dumb boy?"

"Yes, how?" asked Winona. "That's what I'd like to know."

"I will now listen," said Carney, "to any whistles the Sistren care to propose."

The response was a blast of whistles, loud, soft and breathy, in all combinations of notes.

"Wait!" cried Betsy. "Don't decide yet! I've got a wonderful one, but I can't seem to make it come."

She struggled but in vain. The Sistren waited loyally. They clapped her on the back. The sergeant-at-arms brought a glass of water. Still no whistle, and Alice grew tired of waiting.

"How's this?" she asked. Her whistle came clear

and firm: "Dee *Dee* Dee Dee Dee Dee Dee Dee!"

"Oh, that's cute!"

"That's grand."

"Let's take that one."

"Sister Morrison," scribbled Betsy, "proposed a whistle which was whistled and approved as whistled. Sister Root offered a handshake which was shook and approved as shook. Sister K. Kelly offered a salute which was saluted and approved as saluted.

"The Sistren Biscay, T. Kelly and Ray were appointed by the president to look up the matter of pins. A more suitable committee couldn't have been appointed. Sister Ray is especially competent. Long live our wise president!"

The pins, it was decided, when Betsy stopped reading aloud, would be engraved with the Okto Delta symbol, the triangle with a circle inside, such as Tib had drawn on the invitations.

"Gee, I'm important!" Tib said. "I thought up the name and I drew the first Okto Delta sign. What would you all have done if I'd stayed in Milwaukee?"

"I think we ought to entertain the boys," Winona broke in. "After all, there are other girls in school. If we're busy every Saturday night our boys will find someone to take out."

"Freshmen, probably."

"Yes. They certainly fall for the freshmen."

"Maybe they'll get up a fraternity," Betsy suggested.

"Eight boys, to match our sorority."

There was a chorus of approving cheers.

Nobody wanted to play cards that night. Making plans was much more entertaining. They had refreshments—sandwiches, cocoa and whipped-cream cake —and Winona played the piano.

> "*Morning Cy,*
> *Howdy Cy,*
> *Gosh darn, Cyrus, but you're*
> *Looking spry. . . ."*

They barn-danced. They cake-walked. They practised high kicking. Mr. and Mrs. Ray and Margaret came in before it was over, but secret affairs had all been disposed of so their presence didn't matter. They finished the whipped-cream cake, while the fun went on.

Tib stayed all night with Betsy and they talked the evening over jubilantly as they undressed and put on what Betsy, copying Julia, called their "dream robes."

"I never had so much fun in my life," Tib declared. "I'm so glad you thought of making up a sorority."

"It did go over with a bang," Betsy replied.

And it did. It was as great a success as she had hoped it would be.

"Now," she thought with satisfaction, waiting for sleep to come, "I'm going to begin to do things."

10

The Old Pill

SHE DID BEGIN to do things. But they weren't, or at least the first one wasn't, the sort of things that she had in mind. The first effect of Okto Delta in Betsy's life was catastrophic.

The excitement of the girls did not exhaust itself over the weekend, which was filled with feverish telephoning and rushing from house to house to discuss the new organization. The boys beseiged them with questions.

"What does Okto Delta stand for?"

"Don't you wish you knew!"

"Show me the grip. Come on, I won't tell."

"Tony Markham! Don't you know that sororities are secret?"

"Aw, it's only a club!"

"It's nothing whatever like a club," responded the indignant Okto Deltas.

The high school, when it convened on Monday, was as obtuse as Tony. It was accustomed to clubs which sprang up all the time like eager mushrooms, and it didn't know the difference that Greek letters made. It didn't realize at first how exclusive and important sororities were.

The girls enjoyed mystifying everyone.

"Sister Ray!"

"Sister Kelly!"

"Hi there, Sister in Okto Delta!"

"What is this Okto Delta?" fellow students inquired in complete good humor.

"Just wait! You'll find out!"

Betsy, in a line of marchers heading for the Latin class, passed Winona heading for the physics lab. These lines were fairly rigid. Students were not supposed to break away nor pause for conversation. But passing Betsy, the irrepressible Winona gave the Okto Delta whistle, "Dee *Dee* Dee Dee Dee Dee Dee Dee." She leaned out to take Betsy's hand in the Okto Delta grip. She gave the Okto Delta salute, four fingers lifted on either side of her head, and then on a sudden inspiration, crooked the fingers to make horns. Betsy burst out laughing and Miss Erickson, standing at the door of the classroom, regarded her disapprovingly.

Betsy and Tacy, who usually sat side by side, happened to be separated by a desk or two in Latin class. Bursting to tell Tacy about Winona's antics, Betsy raised her hand. Miss Erickson responded coldly, "Yes?"

"May I please speak to Tacy?"

"Certainly not," replied Miss Erickson. "Anything you have to say to Tacy can wait until the end of the period."

Betsy was annoyed. She was not accustomed to being snubbed in the Deep Valley High School. While Miss Erickson was explaining a difficult passage she wrote a note to Tacy.

"Erickson won't let me speak to you, the old pill. But after class I have a joke to tell you. Thy faithful Sister in Okto Delta, Betsy."

Folding this and marking it with Tacy's name, she passed it along the row to Tacy. Miss Erickson slapped her book shut.

"Betsy Ray! You may bring that note to me."

Betsy blushed. She remembered "the old pill" and blushed more deeply still. Of course, Miss Erickson might throw the note in the waste basket without reading it. That, thought Betsy virtuously, would be the honorable thing to do. But she might conceivably read it.

"If she does," thought Betsy defiantly, "it's just too bad."

She took the note, walked to the front of the room and held it out.

To her surprise Miss Erickson didn't take it. Instead she said, "We would all like to know what business you and Tacy have that is important enough to interrupt Cataline's orations. You may read the note to the class."

"Not . . . aloud!" Betsy cried.

"That is what I said," Miss Erickson answered.

"I . . . I'd rather not."

"You should have thought of that before you wrote it."

Betsy turned a still deeper crimson. After a brief, desperate hesitation, she threw off her accustomed droop, stood erect and read: "Erickson won't let me speak to you, the old pill. But after class I have a joke to tell you. Thy faithful Sister in Okto Delta, Betsy."

There was an aghast silence in the Cicero classroom.

Joe Willard, who never reacted like other people, looked amused, but everyone else looked frightened. Tacy was so pale that her freckles stood out.

Betsy glanced furtively toward Miss Erickson. She, too, was blushing. Angry color ran from the edge of her bright yellow hair down to her stiff white collar.

"Betsy," said Miss Erickson, "take that note to Miss Bangeter. Tell her the circumstances under which you read it to the class."

"Yes, ma'am," Betsy replied. She folded the note and went out.

Years seemed to fall away as she stood in the empty hall. She felt as though she were a little girl again in grade school, sent by the teacher to another room with a note. She had been proud then, but she had always felt a little frightened, too.

The hall was surrounded by classrooms from which came the murmur of monotonous voices. There was a water fountain, and she took a drink. She went to the cloakroom mirror and fluffed her hair aimlessly without really looking at her burning face.

Miss Bangeter's office was behind the assembly room. Miss Clarke, in charge of the study period there, smiled brightly as Betsy walked through. Betsy forced a sickly smile in return.

Being sent to Miss Bangeter was a strangely powerful chastisement. She was not unduly severe; she was known to be just and even generous. But she was such an awesome personage, she lived on such Olympian heights that there was a profound humiliation merely in bringing wrongdoing into her presence.

Knocking at the door Betsy reflected that it was the first time she had been sent to the principal's office for a reprimand. She had seen it happen dozens of times to boys and girls she knew. It was always happening to Winona. But Betsy Ray was supposed to be a different kind of person. She was the kind who is elected to class office, who has conferences with the teachers on school affairs, not her own misdemeanors. This was plain in the expression which crossed Miss Bangeter's face when she saw who had entered.

"Yes, Betsy," she said pleasantly. "What is it?"

Betsy's face was still suffused with crimson. She walked slowly and her throat was so dry that she could hardly speak.

"Miss Erickson asked me to give you this note."

"Miss Erickson wrote me a note?" Miss Bangeter sounded puzzled. Obviously she could not understand why Betsy was so perturbed.

"She didn't write it," Betsy said. "I did. I wrote it to Tacy or rather . . ." she paused. "Miss Erickson asked me to tell you the full circumstances, so I'll have to go a little farther back. I asked to speak to Tacy during class and Miss Erickson wouldn't let me."

"Was it about a personal matter?" Miss Bangeter asked judicially.

"Yes," said Betsy. "I couldn't speak to Tacy so I wrote her a note, and Miss Erickson saw me passing it and asked me to bring it to the front and read it out loud. So I did." Betsy gulped. "She told me to bring it to you."

Miss Bangeter accepted the folded paper and laid it aside. She leaned forward, crossing her arms on the desk, looking into Betsy's face with keen, grave eyes. She spoke in a tone of dignified intimacy.

"Just what do you think of all this, Betsy?"

"I think I acted very foolishly, but I think, too—" Betsy's tone grew resentful, and she paused.

"I know," said Miss Bangeter, "you think that Miss Erickson shouldn't have read your note. But you must take into consideration that she is a young, inexperienced teacher. She's just out of college, you know.

"Before you judge Miss Erickson, I suggest that you judge yourself. Wasn't it impudent to write a note after you had been refused permission to speak? Shouldn't you have accepted Miss Erickson's ruling not to discuss this matter with Tacy during class? Couldn't it have waited anyway? Was it really important?"

Betsy felt tears come into her eyes. She cried easily,

disgustingly so, she always thought. She was resolved not to cry now so she dared not speak. She clamped her jaws so firmly that she looked like a squirrel stuffed with nuts. Reaching out she opened the note and spread it in front of Miss Bangeter.

Miss Bangeter read it. A lightning flicker of amusement was gone so quickly that Betsy was not positive she had seen it, although she thought she had and it cheered her up a little.

"What do you think you ought to do?" Miss Bangeter asked.

"Go back and apologize, I suppose," muttered Betsy.

"Right," returned the principal crisply. "And I should say that it ought to be in front of the class. Don't you think so? Since the whole class heard the note?"

Betsy nodded. She got up. "Thank you, Miss Bangeter," she said and slipped miserably out the door.

Back in the cloakroom she looked into the mirror, with purpose this time. She ran her back comb through her hair, rubbed a chamois skin over her nose. She returned to the drinking fountain and took another drink. She reached the door of Miss Erickson's room, but she stood so long without opening it that it seemed to her she had been standing there for years and would be there forever. At last, with false briskness, she turned the knob.

Silence fell as she entered. Cicero's finest oratorical flights could not compete with this.

"Miss Erickson," said Betsy. But she looked at Tacy who was staring down, suffering. She turned determinedly and faced Miss Erickson. "I'm very sorry that I was impudent," she said in a firm voice.

"Did Miss Bangeter tell you to apologize to me?"

"No, ma'am," said Betsy. "But I told her I was going to."

"Very well," said Miss Erickson. "Your apology is accepted. But I will not let you be tempted to write more notes. You may move down to this front seat. Hazel will change with you. She can be trusted in the back row."

Hazel Smith was a friendly, freckle-faced girl whom Betsy liked. She looked sheepish as she carried her books back to Betsy's old seat. Betsy took her own load of books and moved to the front seat, another common indignity which she now received for the first time in her life.

It was a minor sensation around school, Betsy Ray calling Miss Erickson a pill, being sent to the principal, being moved to a front seat. Betsy acted jaunty about it, especially with the girls after school.

"After all," she said, "I was just living up to Okto

Delta. You know that fatal D!"

She told the story at the supper table, and Mrs. Ray was indignant with Miss Erickson.

"I never heard of such a thing," she said. "You learn in kindergarten that you don't read other people's mail."

"It's kindergarten stuff," said Mr. Ray, "that school isn't for writing notes, passing notes, receiving notes, reading notes, or anything else of that nature."

"You're right," Betsy admitted glumly. She felt extremely foolish. Okto Delta had started out wrong. It was different than she had thought it would be. It didn't seem to tie up with those plans she had made for the winter.

Those fine lofty plans came to vivid life a few days later when the family drove out to Murmuring Lake. Mr. and Mrs. Ray had been married there, at Pleasant Park across the lake from the Inn, and weather permitting they made this romantic pilgrimage every October fifteenth.

This year the day was red-gold and crisp. The Inn was festive under scarlet vines but a big stove crackled in the almost empty dining room. Mrs. Van Blarcum hurried in and out, and Mr. Van Blarcum, with plenty of time to spare as usual, chatted with them while they ate the traditionally magnificent dinner.

Afterwards, while Mr. Ray smoked his cigar, Betsy ran down to say hello to Pete. She couldn't find him, but standing on the dock she looked across the cool, twinkling water to Babcock's Bay and thought about the day she had sat in a rowboat there and mapped out her winter.

She had resolved, first of all, to try to take Julia's place. She hadn't, she admitted, done very well at that. She was almost never at home, and she remembered, with a twinge, rebuffing Margaret on the day she and Tacy and Tib planned Okto Delta.

She had resolved to excel in school, to become a leader, and instead she had had a quarrel with Miss Erickson. Joe Willard had dropped out of her plans, too, but that wasn't her fault.

"Anyhow, what's Joe Willard to me? I'm getting plenty of attention from boys this year," Betsy said aloud. She went on in her thoughts, "The only thing I've stuck to is my music. And I don't think I have a shred of talent for it. Of course—I invented Okto Delta. . . ."

That hadn't helped so far, though. It had even hindered.

She frowned at the distant blur of yellow cottonwood trees rimming Babcock's Bay and with intense concentration re-established in her mind the pattern she had set for her winter: thoughtfulness at home, good work at school, piano lessons. . . .

"And now," she added, "making something out of Okto Delta . . . something good."

She held Margaret's hand cozily during the afternoon ramble around Pleasant Park. As usual, with her father smiling in calm content and her mother vivaciously explaining, they visited the oak tree under which the two had become engaged. They stood in the bay window where the marriage had taken place, and had tea with the wife of the farmer who now owned the house.

Although they all missed Julia, they had a happy, satisfying time. And driving home Betsy told Margaret stories. At last, lulled by the beat of Old Mag's hoofs and the rhythmic creaking of the wheels, they sank into drowsy silence.

Betsy's thoughts went back to her plans for the winter. If a sorority was going to be any help, it must be a little more serious. Epsilon Iota, which Julia hoped so much to join, sounded very serious. But Okto Delta hadn't turned out that way.

"I must, I must, bring out the serious side," thought Betsy, rolling through the dark.

11

"Hence, Loathed Melancholy!"

MAKING OKTO DELTA SERIOUS was certainly uphill work.

The juniors in the sorority, who were studying Foundations of English Literature under Miss Fowler, had made the acquaintance of Milton's poems, "L'Allegro" and "Il Penseroso." Winona stalked into every Okto Delta meeting flinging up a long arm and crying,

"Hence, loathed Melancholy!" And the Sistren would chant in uproarious sing-song:

> *"Haste-thee-nymph-and-bring-with-thee-*
> *Jest-and-youth-ful-Joll-i-tee-*
> *Quips-and-cranks-and-wan-ton-Wiles-*
> *Nods-and-Becks-and-Wreath-ed-Smiles . . ."*

If Betsy ever shouted, "Hence, vain deluding joyes!" her voice was certainly drowned out in the racket.

But it is doubtful that she ever shouted, in spite of the good resolutions she had made riding home from Murmuring Lake. She relished the flattering laughter that arose when she read the minutes of the meetings.

"The second meeting of the Okto Delta sorority was held on October seventeenth at the home of Sister Root. The meeting was called to order by the president, and the Sistren showed undue mirth and hilarity during the reading of the minutes. (The secretary-treasurer is very witty, as well as pretty and good.)

"The appointed committee reported on the subject of pins. Sistren Biscay, T. Kelly and Ray had conducted this matter with their usual efficiency, and a local jewelry store is now engraving eight gold pins with the mystic Okto Delta symbols. The price of the pins should not cause fathers undue suffering for they are a mere one dollar per. They will be delivered shortly and will doubtless cause a sensation in the Deep Valley High.

"Sister Morrison moved that the meetings always be held in the afternoon. She was hooted down and didn't mind at all; it had been her mother's idea, anyway. Sister K. Kelly suggested a cross-country tramp for the following Thursday. This was agreed upon, one of her chocolate cakes being part of the bargain.

"Sister Root proposed opening the sorority to boys. This also was hooted down. Sister T. Kelly, who doesn't like boys, grew as red as her own locks with rage. Sister Root would have been abashed if she had been anyone but Sister Root. 'Let them get up a fraternity of their own,' said the wise secretary-treasurer.

"After this business meeting, conducted with skill and dispatch by our honored president, the Sistren brought out sewing bags, and their lily-white fingers flashed as they crocheted, tatted, embroidered, or just plain sewed. Sister Ray worked on the world's most famous jabot, destined for Sister Sibley's swan-like neck. They also toasted marshmallows and discussed important matters: to wit, boys.

"Sistren T. Kelly, Muller, Root and Ray gave a drama in one act entitled, *Woman versus Woman*, or *She Loved but Killed Him*. The actors were superb. The audience watched the brilliant portrayal of love and hatred with tense faces, swayed from tears to laughter.

"The Sistren were then served with a delicious lunch. They are noted for their delicate appetites, but on this occasion they unbent and really ate. The meeting then adjourned."

This meeting was described, a trifle more formally, in Winona's father's paper, the *Deep Valley Sun*. There was a good deal of talk about Okto Delta around school next day.

On the following week the sorority met with Carney.

"The Sistren didn't have a very successful business meeting for they were disturbed by the male element, including Dave Hunt. (The secretary-treasurer writes this name with a delicate blush; she thinks he's cute.) After an unladylike chase over the Sibley premises and the capture of several trophies, including Cab Edward's cap, the Sistren returned to the house and henceforth the male element inspected proceedings from the windows.

"The minutes of the previous meeting were read and objected to, although it has slipped my mind entirely why. I am sure it was a silly objection as Sister Ray always writes up the minutes in a concise, dignified manner, and no legitimate objection could possibly be found. Sister Biscay handed out the new pins and with difficulty collected a dollar from each member.

"After the business meeting the Sistren played cards. To find their partners they drew sticks of licorice tied with orange bows. For a head prize Sister Sibley gave an orange and black pincushion and for a consolation prize a lemon.

"When the delectable refreshments were served, Sister Root again brought up the matter of inviting boys into the order and seemed to receive some support from Sister Muller, who is too small to have any weight in such discussions. Both of them were sternly rebuked. Sister Sibley, our noble president, announced that she has learned to drive her father's auto and will take the Sistren in a body to the St. John game."

This meeting likewise was written up, in a slightly different vein, by the *Deep Valley Sun*, and the high school looked with interest at the gold pins, engraved with a triangle having a circle inside, which appeared on eight shirt waists the following Monday.

"Sister Biscay entertained the Okto Deltas at a particularly skippy luncheon. Places at the table were marked by clothes pin dolls dressed in orange and black. Five hundred was played, with only a few interruptions in the form of fist fights, ragtime, Sister Muller's 'Baby Dance,' and the 'Cat Duet' sung with feeling and some masterly caterwauls by Sistren T. Kelly and Ray. The head prize was won by Sister

Morrison. It was a peachy little doll dressed in an orange and black princesse dress. The booby prize, won by Sister Muller, consisted of a soap teddy bear. A gentle hint, Sister Muller!

"Sister Root insisted at the top of her voice that if we won't let the boys join, we simply must entertain them. Sister Muller seconded the motion, although anyone as small as she is should be seen and not heard. Then Sister K. Kelly, a genius of the first order, quieted everyone with a terrific announcement.

"She said that it was the Sistren Kellys' turn to entertain next time and that, since there were two of them, it would be only fair for them to entertain twice as many people. Therefore, each girl might invite a boy.

"Great was the rush for Sister Biscay's telephone, and the Sistren, who are well known for their beauty, charm and initiative, especially initiative, had no difficulty in ensnaring eight hapless males. This party will occur on the night of the St. John game to which Sister Sibley will take us in her auto. It should be quite a day."

It was. The St. John game was always the climax of the football season in Deep Valley. Excitement would have mounted in all breasts even though there had been no Okto Delta plans afoot. But these grew more sensational all the time.

Tib danced up to Betsy, Tacy and Carney in the Social Room.

"I have some of that cardboard left over from the invitations, and those orange and black crayons. Wouldn't you like to have me make an Okto Delta poster to put on the front of Carney's auto?"

The response was enthusiastic:

"Marvelous."

"Let's make an Okto Delta pennant, too."

"How about some orange and black arm bands?"

"Maybe," Carney suggested, "we ought to wear the school colors?"

"Oh, sure! But we could combine them with the Okto Delta colors."

"Let's all dress alike."

"What shall it be? Sweaters and tams? Gee, I wish we had black sweaters and orange tams!"

"Maybe next year. . . ." Betsy began, but Carney interrupted.

"Don't make me feel bad. Next year I'll be at Vassar."

"Just think!" cried Betsy. "You'll be an alumnus, the very first Okto Delta alumnus!"

"Betsy!" said Carney. "We're females, and the word is alumna."

"It's alumnae, I think," Tib interrupted earnestly. "I've never studied Latin but I used to hear them use that word at Browner."

"Oh, let's just say alum," said Betsy. "It sounds more casual, anyway. You will be the first Okto Delta alum."

On the day of the game the eight girls met at the

Sibleys', all wearing sweaters and tams with orange and black arm bands and carrying an Okto Delta pennant. Tib had made a huge Okto Delta poster which they fastened to the front of the automobile. Mr. and Mrs. Sibley laughed at these arrangements but their main interest was in Carney's manipulation of the steering wheel. She had been practising driving for two months now and was almost as proficient as her father, who still relapsed occasionally into "Giddap!" and "Whoa!"

It was an overcast day in November. The trees had been stripped of their last withered leaves. Winter was sharpening its knives, but Okto Delta made its own warmth as the girls, flushed and laughing, crowded into the automobile.

Carney's brother cranked the machine, which began to quiver and make explosive noises. Shortly it was rolling down Front Street, where the gaudy sign on the front, the pennant, waved by Tib sitting on Winona's lap, all the bright colors and frenzied cheering caused the most insensitive passers-by to stop, look and listen.

Waving and cheering, the Okto Deltas rode on to the football field at the edge of town. There were no stands. Spectators usually stood or walked up and down the side lines. Occasionally someone watched from a buggy or an automobile, but this wasn't considered sporting.

The Okto Deltas were full of school spirit, and after their spectacular arrival had been fully appreciated they piled out of the car.

Hazel Smith caught sight of Betsy, waved and started toward her. Then she noticed the display of sweaters and tams, the orange and black colors, the new pins gleaming. Trying to act as though she had been heading somewhere else, she angled away.

"Hi, Hazel!" Betsy cried. "Come on over!"

Hazel came, but diffidently.

"Stay and watch the game with us," Betsy said. She shouldn't have said it. It had been agreed that the Okto Deltas were going to remain as a unit throughout the whole game. But she thought Hazel looked odd.

"No," said Hazel, "I'm with somebody else. Is this your new club? Pretty skippy, aren't you?" She said it good naturedly, but Betsy was troubled by the speed with which she ducked away.

The Okto Deltas had no difficulty watching the game as a unit, at least so far as girls were concerned. No other girls approached them. Most of the boys they knew were either on the football team or among the scrubs who were also in uniform, hoping to be called as replacements. Lloyd Harrington wasn't on the team and he joined Tib at once, remaining beside her to instruct and explain. Tib was an excellent vacant-lot football player herself, but she asked naive questions and listened round-eyed.

Another boy on the side lines was Joe Willard.

Joe had never been able to go out for football because he worked after school. Heretofore, he had not been able even to come to the games. But he was here today as representative of the *Deep Valley Sun*. Bareheaded, wearing a heavy blue turtle-neck sweater, a swatch of yellow copy paper stuck in his hip pocket, he dashed up and down the side lines abreast of the battling teams. His face was glowing with excitement and Betsy remembered Cab telling her last year that Joe was good at football. He could have been an outstanding athlete, Stewie, the coach, had said. Joe had never seemed to mind not having time for athletics. He had said offhandedly that he would play in college. But watching him now, Betsy realized that it must have been a real deprivation.

Just as the first half ended without a score, Joe's peregrinations brought him upon the Okto Deltas. They were standing in front of their decorated auto.

"Hey, what's all this?" he asked, looking at Betsy.

"Haven't you heard about the new sorority? I thought you were expected to keep up with the news." Betsy smiled saucily, glad that there were plenty of curls pulled out beneath her tam.

"Only important news. What's the name of the thing?"

"Okto Delta. Greek letters, you know."

"Greek letters?" Joe looked puzzled. "I got ambitious and tried to learn some Greek one time. Okto isn't a letter; it's a word."

"Oh, don't be like Gaston," said Betsy. "The effect is Greek letters."

"The effect," said Joe, his blue eyes roving over the group, "is kind of cute," with which remark he sauntered off. The disgustingly general compliment gave Betsy no pleasure. He was freer with compliments these days, which meant, in her opinion, that they were meaningless. She would have preferred the pretended insults she was sure he heaped on Phyllis.

The Okto Deltas, eight strong, began to shout:

> "We'll whoop her up for D. V.
> We've got 'em on the run,
> We're going to beat St. John's boys,
> And the fun is just begun.
> There's Larson, Hunt and Edwards,
> They'll hit that line a few,
> With such an aggregation,
> We won't do much to you."

Betsy shouted along with the rest, but her eyes followed Joe's retreating figure.

Phyllis Brandish was sitting in her auto. He joined her and sat there until the second half. When he got out, she followed, a chic, distinctive figure in a russet red suit, fur boa and muff. Furs were the rage that year. For a while she accompanied him in his rovings up and down the field. At last, with a small intimate wave of her hand which seemed to say that she couldn't keep up with him, she retired to her auto again.

In the second half each team made a touchdown. Then Dave Hunt, providentially long-legged, kicked a goal and Deep Valley won the game. The clamor was terrific. Joe Willard was bellowing like a madman. The Okto Deltas were screaming and jumping and hugging one another, and Betsy acted as frantic as everyone else. Yet she didn't feel particularly happy.

She looked beyond the joy-crazed crowd to the naked brown trees on the horizon. She noticed the long, grave bands of cloud in the west. She was aware that Joe had dashed to Phyllis' auto, cranked it and climbed in. It lumbered across the field, then flew down the road, taking the story of Deep Valley's triumph to the waiting presses. She felt depressed as she swayed lightly with her arms on the shoulders of the other girls, singing, "Cheer, cheer, the gang's all here."

"Wasn't Dave Hunt wonderful?"

"Marvelous!"

"I've yelled until I'm hoarse."

Not only the Okto Deltas but almost the entire student body returned up Front Street blowing horns, ringing bells, cheering, singing and yelling. The team went into the Y.M.C.A. for showers and rub downs but the hullabaloo continued in the street outside. Nearby delicatessens were raided for nourishment. The Okto Deltas secured jelly doughnuts and cream puffs.

"I dare you to give a cream puff to that policeman," Tacy challenged Winona.

"Sure. Why not?" Black eyes shining and white teeth gleaming, Winona loped over to Patrolman Reardon who accepted the squashy pastry with a grin.

The uproar continued, but Katie said, "Tacy and I have to go home if we're going to give a party tonight."

"Well, you're giving a party all right. A pretty important one, the first Okto Delta party with boys."

"We must all go home and start dressing."

"But I want to wait and see the team!" Tib cried, protesting.

Carney laughed. "Almost the whole team is coming to our party: Al, Squirrelly, Cab, Dennie. It's too bad Dave Hunt isn't in the Crowd."

But Dave Hunt hadn't yet started taking out girls. He looked at them with his serious dark blue eyes, but he didn't talk to them. Nobody even suggested that he was afraid. Dave Hunt was afraid of nothing. He would start taking girls out when he was good and ready, everyone agreed.

12

Agley-er and Agley-er

Tib went home with Betsy. She had brought her "dream robe" to the Rays before the game and would return to stay all night after the party. She and Betsy burst in late for supper, windblown, ruddy, hoarse, but ecstatic.

"What did you think of the game, Mr. Ray?— Wasn't it wonderful?—Wasn't it divine?"

He forgave them for being late and Anna reheated their supper. Mrs. Ray and Margaret sat with them while they ate, listening to extravagant accounts of the Deep Valley football team's prowess.

It was almost like having Julia home again to have Tib dressing with Betsy for the party. Returning from the bathroom, freshly bathed and fragrant with talc, they laced up one another's corsets. Betsy had just started wearing a corset. Her mother had brought it to her after a trip to the cities to visit Julia. Tib's waist measured only eighteen inches but she urged Betsy to pull on the laces to make it smaller still.

Margaret brought Washington in to watch and Mrs. Ray darted in and out, as Betsy and Tib made elaborate toilets, talking, laughing, borrowing, lending, squinting into hand mirrors, revolving before the long glass.

Tib had made black and orange bows for them to wear in their hair.

"I'll do your hairs for you, Betsy," she offered. One of Tib's small Germanisms was saying "hairs" for "hair."

"All of them? Which ones?" Betsy teased her.

"Hair! Hair! Ach, will I never remember?"

She fluffed Betsy's hair over the wire "jimmy" into an airy pompadour.

Betsy was taking Tony to the party. She liked him

better than any other boy, although they were definitely on a brother-sister basis. He wasn't going with
the Crowd so much this year. He had always seemed
more mature than the others, and his new friends
were older boys, who were out of school and considered a little wild. With the Rays, however, he was the
same loyal, teasing, affectionate Tony. And he seldom
failed to appear for Sunday night lunch.

Earlier in the season Betsy had thought it would be
perfect if Tony would start going with Tib. She had
hinted this to Tony but without success.

"Aw, she's still playing with doll clothes!" he
would say, indulgently scornful. He patted Tib on her
yellow head, swung her off the floor like a child. He
was definitely not impressed.

But E. Lloyd Harrington was impressed. He had
showered her with attentions and Tib had recipro-
cated by inviting him to the party tonight.

He called for them in his father's auto. Tony
cranked, then climbed into the back seat beside Betsy,
while Lloyd, with Tib at his side, proudly grasped the
wheel. The cold wind blew past their faces and Betsy
was glad that her carefully constructed coiffure was
tied in place with a party scarf.

The Kellys lived in a sprawling old white house at
the end of Hill Street. Betsy had lived in a yellow cottage opposite for the first fourteen years of her life.

Beyond these two houses, which ended the street, hills spread in a half open fan. They were brown and bleak tonight under the cold bright stars.

Betsy was pleased to be arriving in Lloyd's auto when she saw Irma alighting from Phil's machine. Inside the house there were black and orange decorations, and Winona was pounding on the piano.

Betsy was soon encircled. She was joyfully aware that she attracted boys more easily this year. Even Phil was looking at her with interest and when someone started to play "The Merry Widow Waltz," which had woven itself through their romance last spring, he came over to her.

She looked up at him, widening her eyes into what she hoped was a soulful gaze.

"I wondered whether you would come."

"Did you, really?"

"As long as I live I'll never hear 'The Merry Widow Waltz' without thinking of you."

They danced, and Betsy's dancing was one of her strong points. He was so fascinated that Irma was obliged to make an effort to recall him. True, it wasn't much of an effort. It was hardly more than lifting her finger. But to force Irma to any sort of effort was a triumph. She attracted simply by existing, a fact which continued to exasperate her Sistren in Okto Delta.

The success of the party was surpassed only by the terrific success of the refreshments. Everyone always looked forward to refreshments at the Kelly house. Tactfully seizing a moment when Katie's chocolate cake, smothered with thick fudge frosting, was being cut, the girls said what fun it would be if the boys got up a fraternity.

Lloyd seemed to like the idea. "We could have a fraternity house like the boys have up at the U. My Dad's made our barn into a garage, and there are a couple of rooms above it. I have a phonograph up there and some books. It would make a swell club-house."

Tony scoffed. "I don't like fraternities. Too many fellows left out. Besides, I wouldn't tie myself down about what I'm going to do every Saturday night."

But for a number of Saturday nights following the Kellys' party, boys, as well as girls, were busy with Okto Delta. Okto Delta meetings were practically parties, parents complained. Tib didn't complain. Just out of a girl's school, away from the strict influence of *Grosspapas* and *Grossmamas*, she was intoxicated with the freedom of life in Deep Valley. Tib, who could cook and sew, who had always been famous for her practicality and common sense, now thought of nothing but fun.

She and Betsy pursued it together. Tacy would have

been a welcome third but she wasn't interested in boys. She enjoyed hearing Betsy and Tib talk about their adventures, the plots and counterplots by which they proposed to snare this boy or that, but she took no share in such enterprises. She was studying singing with Mrs. Poppy; that was romance enough for her.

This was in November, when waves of ducks were passing through Minnesota on their way to the north country. Mr. Muller and Fred went hunting every Saturday, and Betsy took to going home with Tib after church for Sunday dinner: duck with apple dressing, dumplings, brown gravy, served with butter-drenched sweet potatoes and often topped off by apple pie which came to the table under a crown of whipped cream.

After these succulent feasts they sat in Tib's room and talked.

They talked about clothes, about the new princesse style party dresses they were having made for the holidays, about the furs—like Phyllis Brandish's—they hoped they would get for Christmas. They talked about face powders and finger nail polishes. They talked about perfumes. But especially they talked about boys.

Betsy, having seen so much of boys during the past two years, didn't think they were quite so wonderful as Tib did, but she considered them important. Like most high school girls, she wanted more than almost anything else to be popular with boys. And this year she could call herself that. Of course, she didn't have Irma's magic appeal nor Julia's devastating effect, but she had a little more than her share of attention.

She was gratified to discover that she could hold her own with Tib. Tib was so pretty, so enchanting, so beautifully dressed, Betsy wouldn't have been surprised nor even very resentful if Tib had put her in the shade. But she didn't. It was true that the boys who liked Tib thought of Betsy only as Tib's best friend, but it was equally true that the boys who liked Betsy found Tib merely "cute." Like Tony, they patted her on the head and forgot her. Just as Betsy had foreseen long ago in Milwaukee, she and Tib made an excellent team.

They often spoke of Dave Hunt, the most desirable unattached boy in school. Last summer at the lake, Betsy had thought he was drawn to her, but she was beginning to doubt it. She wasn't the only girl he gazed at, and because his blue eyes were so deep-set and serious the gaze seemed to hold more significance than, perhaps, it had.

As for Tib, although she valued the prestige created by Lloyd's admiration, her affections leaned toward Dennie. He was an ingratiating Irish boy with a curly tangle of hair, fuzzy eyebrows and a dimple in his chin. He liked to sing and act the clown. Dennie and Cab, Tib and Betsy made a rollicking foursome.

They planned little parties for four which they called "soirees." Betsy and Tib secretly nicknamed each other Madame DuBarry and Madame Pompadour. They addressed each other as "M.P." and "M.D.," to the boys' mystification. Tib loved to cook dainty little suppers, which she served by candlelight. Betsy enjoyed trying out dishes she had learned in Domestic Science, especially English Monkey, made in a chafing-dish.

They undeniably had fun. School, of course, suffered.

Betsy, Tacy and Tib had let autumn slip into winter without starting their herbariums for botany. The fall flowers were gone, withered and dead beneath the first delicate fall of snow.

"What will we do about it?" Tib asked anxiously.

"We'll just have to find more flowers in the spring. That's when they bloom, tra la."

Dennie gave a hint which retarded their progress in United States History.

"Know what I do when I haven't got my lesson? I yawn. Clarke always has to yawn back and when she gets started she can't stop. It slows things up a lot."

Betsy tried it and was fascinated by her success. Miss Clarke yawned so prettily, too, tapping her lips with white, almond-tipped fingers.

Miss Erickson couldn't be persuaded to yawn, and Betsy was cold to the eloquence of Cicero.

She worked for Miss Fowler in Foundations of English Literature but so far Miss Fowler hadn't given her exceptionally high marks. Her stories and essays were returned critically marked up with red pencil.

One day Miss Fowler asked her to stay after class. The little Bostonian looked up at Betsy with her very bright dark eyes.

"Betsy," she said in that odd accent like Miss Bangeter's, "I want to tell you a secret. Can you keep a secret?"

"Why, yes."

"You may have noticed that I am harder on you than on the others. I'm harder on you and Joe Willard. And I want you to know the reason why. It's because you have more talent than the others." She paused, then added earnestly, "I think you have a real gift for writing, and I'd like to help you develop it."

Betsy was so taken aback that she could hardly speak.

"I'd like to have you do that, Miss Fowler," she faltered. She blushed like a freshman. "I'll work hard."

Miss Fowler smiled. "I said the same thing to Joe. You two are going to be picked on."

After this Betsy worked even harder on Foundations

of English Literature. And she enjoyed the Girls Debating Club which argued in November that "Immigration should be further restricted." She and Hazel Smith were given the affirmative side. The more Betsy saw of Hazel the better she liked her. It would be fun, she thought, to have her at a party. But this was not immediately possible for she gave so many Okto Delta parties that she couldn't very well have the ordinary kind.

She continued to work hard on her music. She practised daily and looked forward to her lessons, although she felt increasingly sure that, in this field, she had no talent. But she liked Miss Cobb and her visits to the small, warm, geranium-scented house.

Always sociable, Betsy fell into the habit of going into the back parlor after her lessons and talking with Leonard. He liked to hear about Okto Delta, and leaning his bright head on a frail hand, his eyes smiling and his cheeks flushed, he listened to Betsy's stories about the meetings.

Last year at this time he had been out on the football field. This year his illness was so pronounced that his aunt talked of sending him to Colorado. Betsy remembered that his older brother and sister had already died of this disease, and she tried to make the Okto Delta meetings sound even funnier than they were.

"I wish you came for a lesson every day," Leonard told her, weak from laughter.

"You'd be practically an Okto Delta if I did. You're getting to know all the secrets of our order."

Leonard approved of Okto Delta, one of the few outside the membership who did.

Julia came home for Thanksgiving. The train swept down the track with a special brilliance because it carried Julia. She alighted looking citified, and soon filled the Ray house with color and excitement.

She had joined the Dramatic Club. She had been singing solos everywhere. Roger Tate was coming for the weekend.

She brought all the newest songs.

> *"You are my Rose of Mexico,*
> *The one I loved so long ago. . . ."*

The Crowd harmonized richly, standing around the piano. Tom Slade's violin accompanied them, for he had arrived from Cox Military, bringing, as usual, the latest slang. "Ain't it awful, Mabel!" reverberated through the Crowd.

The Rays and the Slades always had Thanksgiving dinner together. It was at the Ray house this year and was followed about twilight by Mr. Ray's turkey sandwiches and coffee, and Grandma Slade's stories.

Listening to these from a pillow in front of the fire, Betsy saw canoes on the river, the raw log cabins of the earliest settlers straggling along the river bank, the Indian Agency at the top of Agency Hill and the Indians coming to take possession of it. They had come in canoes and in dog carts, riding ponies and on foot; a picturesque invasion; not terrifying like the one some years later, when red men came down the Valley pillaging, burning and killing. Deep Valley, now so peaceful, had been a perilous frontier.

The day after Thanksgiving Roger arrived. With his padded shoulders and condescending air, he cut a swath in Deep Valley. Betsy didn't like him very well, although he brought her a fraternity pennant. Julia still gazed at him with the soulful look her sister tried to imitate, yet Betsy felt sure his time was running out.

He and Julia talked about Greek letter organizations. Four sororities were rushing Julia now, but she still preferred Epsilon Iota.

"You're an Epsilon Iota type," Roger assured her profoundly.

Of course, she couldn't be asked to join until spring, but the girls were still showering her with subtle attentions—sweet notes, wee bouquets, affectionate strolls on the campus.

Roger had asked her to wear his fraternity pin.

Julia explained this college custom to Betsy.

"It's almost like being engaged to wear a man's fraternity pin. I won't wear Roger's—I don't like him well enough. But pins certainly change hands fast up at the U."

Betsy rushed to Tib, "Let's let Cab and Dennie wear our Okto Delta pins. Just for a few days, to cause a sensation."

It caused a sensation indeed. Hurt and indignant, Lloyd wrote Tib a scathing note; she countered with a cold one; he wrote back terminating their romance.

"Ain't it awful, Mabel!" Tib said pertly.

They made up, and Lloyd started wearing her pin. Squirrelly had acquired Winona's and Tony was wearing Betsy's now.

The winter grew increasingly chaotic; it wasn't at all what Betsy had planned.

"My plans," she told Tacy, without perceptible regret, "are going agley-er and agley-er."

13
The Curling Iron

IN DECEMBER THE SNOW deepened, the ice on the river thickened, trees snapped with cold and sleigh bells were heard in the streets. As always when winter set in, the tempo of life quickened. Just as people walked faster to stir up their blood against the cold, so they threw themselves, with a sort of defiance, into a host of activities—lodge dances, church bazaars and suppers, club affairs, thimble bees.

Betsy and her mother went Christmas shopping. Betsy bought stickpin holders for the Okto Deltas, and her mother bought fine handkerchiefs on which she would sew lace for the High Fly Whist Club ladies.

Betsy, Tacy and Tib too went on their traditional Christmas shopping trip. It was glorious to have Tib back for that. Three abreast they swung along a crowded, festive Front Street. Their laughter froze above their lips into white clouds.

As when they were children, they shopped for everything: jewels, perfumes, toys, furs—especially furs this year. Yet they broke with the past. They made some purchases besides the Christmas tree ornaments which had once been the sole glittering purpose of the trip.

"We're growing up and I don't like it," said Tacy, as they sat in Heinz's later, drinking coffee.

"We *are!*" Betsy leaned forward suddenly, tense. "*Look* at us sitting here drinking coffee! Just look!"

Tib and Tacy, moved by earnestness, looked into the mirror which ran along the wall.

They saw three girls wearing big, stylish, top-heavy hats. Betsy's was covered with green wings. They had laid off their coats and their shirt waists were trim and snowy. Their finger nails were polished.

"I don't see anything so special," Tib remarked.

"Why, we're sitting here drinking coffee," Betsy repeated somewhat lamely. "And not just for a lark."

Tacy's thoughts followed hers.

"We're actually juniors," she said, "stopping in for coffee after shopping, not freshmen or sophomores pretending to be juniors stopping in for coffee after shopping."

Tib looked confused. "You usually take chocolate," she said. "I've just got you in the habit of coffee because I come from Milwaukee."

"But Tib!" Betsy cried. "That isn't the point. The point is that we're so frightfully old."

"We might have husbands waiting at home," said Tacy.

"Wanting their suppers," added Betsy.

"Oh, it's not that bad!" answered Tib and they all began to laugh.

"Anyway, we have packages to carry," said Tacy, reaching for her coat.

Packages began to pile up in drawers and closets at the Ray house. Carols were being practised by the choir. Betsy wondered what gave these songs their magic. One strain could call up the quivering expectancy of Christmas Eve, childhood, joy and sadness, the lonely wonder of a star.

Tacy sang at Rhetoricals, too full of Christmas

spirit even to be very frightened. She looked beautiful, Betsy thought, her head, with its heavy auburn braids, thrown back, her blue eyes luminous.

> *"I heard the bells on Christmas day,*
> *Their old familiar carols play,*
> *And wild and sweet the words repeat,*
> *Of Peace on Earth, Good Will to men."*

Betsy and Tib were very proud of her.

The Domestic Science class roasted a chicken. The girls gathered around Miss Benbow while she made the dressing, singed and washed the bird, stuffed it and sewed it up. She slid the pan expertly into the oven.

"Now, while it's roasting, I'll dictate general directions for roasting poultry."

Her voice was monotonous, her treatment of the subject less persuasive than the savory odors emanating from the oven. Betsy's thoughts drifted away.

"Betsy Ray."

"Yes, Ma'am." She roused herself quickly.

"Will you baste the chicken, please?"

Betsy rose slowly. "Baste the chicken!" What did that mean? She knew little about cooking. She walked to the stove slowly and pulled open the oven door.

"Baste the chicken!" But baste was something you did with a needle and thread. Miss Benbow had used a needle and thread when she sewed up the chicken. She wouldn't want it sewn up again though. Anyway, it would be too hot to touch.

Betsy looked around frantically, and Winona mouthed instructions. Tacy lifted an imaginary object, dipped it down and raised it up, over and over again.

"She must mean sewing," Betsy thought desperately.

Her immobility and all the gesturing attracted Miss Benbow's attention.

"What is it, Betsy? Why aren't you basting the chicken?"

"How can I?" Betsy blurted. "I haven't a needle and thread!"

Laughter broke over the classroom. Betsy turned scarlet but she laughed, too, and so did Miss Benbow.

"Tacy," she said. "Show her!"

So Tacy came forward and the gesture which Betsy had interpreted as sewing proved to be spooning delicious juices over the crisply browned bird. Later this provided chicken sandwiches for the first of the Christmas parties.

A bigger one, a dance in Schiller Hall, was planned for the last night of school. Boys were maddeningly slow with their invitations as usual, and the Social Room buzzed with speculation when the last week began.

Betsy revolved her chances. They were fairly good, she thought. But she must look pretty tomorrow. She would wear her new Dutch collar. She was so absorbed in plans when the bell rang and they all marched into the assembly room that she gave only a careless glance to the note lying on her desk.

It was written in pencil on a sheet of notebook paper; it looked ordinary enough. But it should have been illuminated on parchment:

"Dear Betsy: How about the dance next Thursday night? Yrs, Dave."

Betsy read it through and immediately read it through again. She read it once more to savor the heavenly sensation of triumph which filled her. This was nice; it was very nice; it was grand; it was swell.

Fortunately Miss Clarke was in charge of the assembly room. Betsy sped a note of acceptance on its way. She asked permission to speak to Tacy, who hugged her, and to Tib, who smothered a squeal.

All the girls were congratulatory but more than one reminded Betsy that Dave Hunt never spoke.

"I know. I know," she told them blithely. "I'm

memorizing *David Copperfield*. I'm going to recite it to him all the way down to the hall and all the way back."

Tib was going with Lloyd, and Tom, home from Cox Military for vacation, invited Tacy. She didn't accept immediately.

"I'm not sure I want to go," she told Betsy and Tib who leaped upon her indignantly.

"You do too want to go!"

"What's the matter with Tom? He looks stunning in his uniform."

"Oh, I like Tom all right. I just don't like dances."

"You like them when you get there. You accept!"

Tacy was indifferent about the whole affair, but Tib was almost as jubilant as Betsy. This was her first high school dance. Again she came to the Rays for supper, bringing a suitcase. They refused dessert and hurried upstairs, followed, of course, by Margaret and the cat, to dress in a giddy whirl.

They pinned starched ruffles under their corset covers and put on their prettiest petticoats. Petticoats this year were sheath-fitting to the knees, then foamed out into lace. Tib wore peach-colored stockings and Betsy wore red ones. The coveted new princesse dresses, peach-colored and red, were laid out on the bed.

"Now," said Tib. "I'm ready to do your hairs."

"Just a moment," said Betsy. "The bathroom was

so steamy that my curls are coming out. I'll freshen them up a bit."

Slipping into a kimono she raced downstairs.

She chattered gaily to Anna while she heated her curling iron over the gas flame. Still chattering, she wound the front middle strand of hair firmly over the iron.

"Lovey!" Anna interrupted. "What's that I smell?"

"Nothing. There's always a little smell when I curl. . . ." But Betsy lowered the iron quickly and Anna cried "Stars in the sky!" For the front middle strand of hair came along with the iron. It was tightly and beautifully curled around the smoking tongs. On her forehead there was only a charred fringe.

With a scream Betsy ran out of the kitchen. Her father rushed in from the parlor holding his newspaper and Margaret, Mrs. Ray and Tib clattered down the stairs.

"My hair! My hair! I can't go to the party!" Betsy burst into tears.

Her mother embraced her. "Of course, you can go."

"No, I can't. I know I can't."

"Let me look, *Liebchen*," Tib commanded.

Mrs. Ray stepped back and Tib smoothed the singed ends with small, artistic fingers.

"I know what we can do. We'll part your hair in the middle and make the pompadour on either side and in back. That's the very newest fashion. The burned part will make sort of a bang."

"This reminds me of *Little Women*," said Margaret. "Remember how Jo burned Meg's hair?"

Betsy blew her nose and wiped her eyes, and they all went back to the kitchen where Tib, standing on tiptoe, took personal charge of the curling. Anna kept saying consolingly that Betsy was going to look puny—her own baffling word for pretty—and Mrs. Ray declared that it wouldn't surprise her at all to see Betsy start a fashion for bangs.

Betsy was laughing now.

"I doubt that," she said, "but at least it will give me something to talk about to Dave."

She was glad to have an anecdote in reserve when Dave strode in at eight o'clock. There wasn't a trace of a smile on his sober, hollow-eyed face.

"He must admit I look nice," Betsy thought, stealing glances in the music room mirror at a vivid, slender, dark-haired girl in a new red princesse dress.

He shook hands with her parents, held her coat and took her party bag, all in silence. Lloyd arrived but the weather was too cold for an automobile, so the two couples started off, walking. Lloyd and Tib soon dropped behind leaving Betsy to her fate.

There wasn't a word from the towering figure that moved in the darkness beside her. She mentioned

Murmuring Lake. No response. She tried to draw him out about the night he put the pennant on the roof. No success. Direct questions received laconic monosyllables.

"All right," thought Betsy, "if he wants me to do all the talking I'll do it." And she started talking about how she had burned her hair. She made it sound as funny as she could, but he didn't laugh. He was as mute as a post. She spun the subject out vivaciously with comparisons of girls' hair and boys' hair, girls' clothes and boys' clothes, and they found themselves at Schiller Hall.

"How did you get along?" Tacy and Tib whispered in the dressing room.

"Why it's unbelievable!" Betsy gasped. "He never said one word! Not a syllable!"

"But you can always talk, Betsy. You're an awful talker and he's *so* good-looking."

He was. When the girls came out into the shining ballroom, Dave was waiting, and Betsy's heart leaped up when she saw him, so tall, so straight, so dramatically stern. Without speaking, of course, he wrote his name three times on Betsy's program.

Mamie Dodd, who always played the piano for high school dances, was warming up her fingers with preliminary chords. These intensified the excitement as boys scurried about, seizing girls' programs and scribbling down their names.

Mamie Dodd swung into the opening waltz.

> "*You are my Rose of Mexico,*
> *The one I loved so long ago. . . .*"

Everyone began to dance and Betsy discovered that Dave was a very good dancer. Floating across the floor in his strong, masterful arms, she forgave him for his silence.

Was there anything in the world, she wondered, so much fun as a dance? She two-stepped happily with Cab to "School Days, School Days, Dear Old Golden Rule Days." Tony had asked her for the barn dance. They ran, kicked and sang:

> "*Morning Cy,*
> *Howdy Cy,*
> *Gosh darn, Cyrus, but you're*
> *Looking spry. . . .*"

She and Dennie sang too:

> "*O'Reilly, O'Reilly,*
> *It's a name that is spoken of highly. . . .*"

Betsy often sang as she danced, which helped out now with Dave.

When Mamie Dodd started to play "The Merry Widow Waltz" Phil glanced across the room. Betsy smiled at him sadly. Later they had a schottische together and talked of the old days.

Betsy hardly saw Tib. They were both far too busy for feminine society.

Joe and Phyllis dropped in late, as though at a casual afterthought. Phyllis wasn't dressed for a dance; she was wearing a suit and hat. The other girls' programs had all been filled, of course, so they had to dance exclusively with each other, but they didn't seem to mind.

Betsy watched them over her partner's shoulder. Joe danced springily, as though he were enjoying himself. Phyllis was languid; her upturned smile was teasing.

Betsy rejoiced fiercely that she had come with Dave Hunt . . . "an outstanding boy, a star athlete. Every girl in school has been hoping he would take her out, and for his first date he chose *me*."

But she saw no indication that Joe Willard knew or cared with whom she had come. He smiled at her. He even waved in high good humor. Betsy waved back radiantly.

After the dance everyone went to Heinz's. The Okto Deltas and their escorts pulled four tables together. They made a joyful racket. Dave Hunt's silence was drowned out, but parting from Tib, Betsy whispered, "Now for *David Copperfield*."

She wasn't quite reduced to *David Copperfield*. By discussing every person at the party, every single boy, girl, and chaperone, dancing in general and barn dancing in particular, Schiller Hall as a place in which to dance and Mamie Dodd as a musician, she managed to talk steadily to the steps of her own porch.

When they parted there, she was rewarded. She gave Dave her hand and said, "I had a very nice time." He didn't answer but he held her hand firmly, and his fascinating, unexpected smile flickered across his face.

"So did I. I'll take you to the next dance," he announced.

"Oh—will you?" Betsy cried joyfully. The absurdity of her response didn't dawn on her until she was telling Tib after the boys had left. Then they went off into peals of laughter.

"Oh—will you?" Betsy mimicked, dropping to her knees, lifting her arms beseechingly.

"Betsy! You *dumm kopf*! You are very lucky that he wants to take you again."

School next day was given over to skylarking. Boys were waving mistletoe; the blackboards were decorated with cartoons, slams and jokes. Assembly included a Christmas tree, with Mr. Gaston acting as Santa Claus. One after another various students were called to the platform to receive joke presents.

Suddenly Betsy heard her name. "Will Miss Betsy Warrington Ray Humphreys Markham Edwards Brandish Hunt and so forth please come forward?" She had started down the aisle with the first name. A new one thundered out with every step she took. She reached the platform covered with blushes while the assembly room roared with laughter.

Mr. Gaston, grinning broadly, held a curling iron.

"This," he read loudly, "is to curl the bang now growing on your lily-white, intellectual brow."

Betsy accepted it to hilarious applause.

She acted plagued, of course, and ran down from the platform, ducking her head. But she was really thoroughly pleased. She must be that most desirable object, a "popular" girl. "Popular" with boys, of course.

Before she dropped off to sleep that night, she relived the whole scene, smiling in the darkness.

"It was awfully silly," she thought. "But I'm glad Joe Willard heard that rigamarole of names. It showed him that I wasn't just sitting around home thinking about him."

14

The Strong Silent Type

THE CURLING IRON WASN'T the only joke present
Betsy received that year. There were always joke presents in the Rays' Christmas stockings. Every year
Mrs. Ray received an onion, tastefully wrapped, with
a card from one Henry Tucker, who had once been
her beau. The writing always looked like Mr. Ray's.
Julia's old beaus sent onions, too, and Mr. Ray was

often presented with a worn-out boot or shoe from Helmus Hanson, who ran the rival shoe store. Anna got chunks of coal from Charlie. Empty salmon cans from Washington, old bones from Abie bulged in Margaret's black-ribbed stockings.

This gave a flavor to Christmas morning quite different from Christmas Eve which was solemn and beautiful. By firelight and Christmas-tree light the family sang the old familiar carols. Betsy read from Dickens' *A Christmas Carol*, Margaret recited "'Twas the Night before Christmas," and Julia, grave and reverent, read the story of Jesus' birth out of the book of Luke.

When this was over, they turned out the lights and filled one another's stockings with smothered giggles which anticipated next morning's fun. "Now you all stay in bed until the house is warm," Mr. Ray always said.

In the morning he shook down the furnace, and heat came up through the registers along with the smell of sausages and coffee. After he had kindled a fire in the grate and Anna had set breakfast on the table to be consumed at will, the gong summoned the rest of the family. Each one rushed to the chair which held his stocking.

Theoretically each one unwrapped a gift in turn but it didn't work out that way. Mr. Ray always forgot to open his; he cared more about watching other people open theirs and sat with crossed legs, smiling benevolently, or moved about, gathering up the discarded paper and ribbons, folding what was usable and burning what wasn't. He handed out the larger boxes which were piled under the Christmas tree and kept going to the table to replenish breakfast plates.

"Have another cup of coffee, Jule. Eat another sausage, Betsy. It won't hurt you."

Everyone else snatched at his own gifts, exclaiming and squealing. Julia and Betsy received combing jackets, the latest fad. Lacy and beribboned, they hung on one's bedpost when not in use. Julia raved over a new blue bathrobe. Margaret clasped a teddy bear and *Mary Ware, the Little Colonel's Chum*. Betsy had her eyes on a big oblong box, wrapped in red and green tissue, which lay under the Christmas tree. It was just the right size to hold furs.

Sure enough, when her father reached that box, he brought it to Betsy. She tried to restrain her smile as she untied the ribbons.

"Now what can this be?" she kept saying, never doubting that it was her longed-for set of furs.

She lifted off the cover and found another box inside.

"This is a joke present!" she cried, but she didn't really think so. The second box, she noted hopefully, was plenty big enough for furs.

The second box, however, yielded a third one and the third, a fourth. The boxes were getting too small for furs now, except for a muff, perhaps. This one might hold a muff. . . .

But it didn't. It held a tissue-wrapped package, and that held another, and another.

"Stars in the sky!" Anna kept shouting, throwing her arms up and down.

Betsy, tearing off papers, hid her disappointment under laughter. The family watched her, laughing, too. Margaret watched from her father's knee, one arm around his neck. At the very end Betsy found a ring box.

"You're going to find an elegant ring, lovey," Anna interjected breathlessly. But the box held only a paper. Betsy unfolded it and read, in her father's printing, "HUNT."

"Hunt? Hunt? Dave Hunt?"

"We knew you'd think that," shrieked Margaret, her little freckled face blazing with excitement.

Her father was chuckling so hard that his stomach shook. "I don't see any 'Dave' on that paper. You've got Dave Hunt on the brain."

"But it says 'Hunt.'"

"Yes, 'Hunt.' Need a dictionary?"

Betsy jumped up, scattering the multitude of boxes. She was off like a flash, running upstairs and down, flinging open drawers and closets. Down in the vegetable bin she found a big box, the size of the first one.

Clutching it joyfully, she raced back to the fire and while the family crowded about, she lifted out a set of furs. They were fluffy blue fox, a neck piece, a muff, even a fur hat with a *chou* of green velvet on the side.

"Papa! Mamma!" She rushed about kissing, then ran to the music-room mirror.

She wore them to church later. She went with Julia, who was singing in the choir during Christmas vacation, and with Tony who had unexpectedly expressed a wish to go. The sidewalks were covered with a thin powdering of frost and the snowbanks seemed to have been sprinkled with diamonds.

Tony held an elbow of either girl. He was wearing a new overcoat, and his red Christmas tie looked well with his black eyes.

Betsy smoothed down her boa, reached up to stroke her hat, snuggled her face into the muff.

"Now, now, Miss Ray! Forget those furs and think about church."

"I am thinking about church. I'm thinking how nice I look in my new furs going to church. I just love Christmas!" Betsy added, sliding along the frosty walk.

"So do I," said Julia, "especially at our house. It's shocking how some people manage Christmas—tell each other ahead of time about their presents—no surprises, no suspense, no drama. Papa and Mamma put such a thrill in it."

"Why, I never thought it was Papa and Mamma," said Betsy, sounding puzzled.

"I appreciate our home more since I've been away," said Julia.

"I appreciate the Ray house myself," Tony remarked. "You may notice that I honor it with my presence now and then."

"In spite of the fact," said Betsy, "that you're quite indifferent to the daughters."

"Oh, quite! Quite!"

She grabbed him. "You'll go into that snowdrift. You and your Christmas tie!"

Laughing his deep laugh Tony struggled with her.

"Children, behave!" Julia said.

The church was filled with a spicy fragrance; the altar was luminously white. From her place in the choir Betsy watched Tony fumbling at the pages of the prayer book, hesitantly kneeling and rising. She heard his rich, deep voice in the hymns.

"I just love Tony," she thought to herself.

The text of the sermon came from that chapter in the book of Luke which Julia had read aloud last night— ". . . *because there was no room for them in the Inn.*"

Rev. Mr. Lewis said that the text was symbolical of Jesus' short life on earth and of the attitude of

Christians. He was ever asking for admission into their lives—their business, social and private lives—but he could not remain where there was graft in business, envy and hatred in society or sin in people's hearts. These things crowded him out.

"I'll never forget that sermon," remarked Julia, walking home.

"I liked it, too," Betsy said.

"Our lives can hold just so much. If they're filled with one thing, they can't be filled with another. We ought to do a lot of thinking about what we want to fill them with."

"See here!" said Tony, "I've heard one sermon today." But he didn't mind Julia's preaching; his black eyes were soft.

Betsy thought about it again after dinner, walking down to Miss Cobb's with a present for Leonard. Okto Delta had crowded a good many things out of her winter—reading, friends like Hazel Smith, telling stories to Margaret, even the early service at church she had always loved so much.

"It hasn't hurt my music lessons, nor my work for Miss Fowler. I wrote the best essay in class on The Elizabethan Age."

But she felt dissatisfied, and resolved to make a long list of resolutions when the new year arrived.

By New Year's, however, she had forgotten her

resolution to make resolutions. The holidays struck Deep Valley like a snowball, exploding with soft glitter in all directions. There were family dinners, visits to country relatives, parties for young and old.

Mr. and Mrs. Ray were always on the go, and Julia had a new "college man" down from the cities. He, too, brought Betsy a fraternity pennant. His fraternity was a different one from Roger Tate's.

Roger's successor was one Pat McFadden, a tall, resplendent Irishman with thick black hair, blue-grey eyes and a flattering tongue.

"He used to go with Norma—you know, that stunning blonde Epsilon Iota. And with lots of other girls. I took him away from half the co-eds on the campus," Julia told Betsy.

Betsy could well believe it. She and Tib were so infatuated that Julia was almost obliged to plot to get rid of them as she had when they were children. Even Tacy liked him—perhaps because he was Irish.

"Top of the morning," she would greet him, her blue eyes sparkling. They talked to each other in brogue.

One reason Tacy liked him was that he was a singer. He had a fine baritone voice. The Rays asked him to sing for everyone who dropped in, and the more people who dropped in the better he liked it. He usually sang the Toreador song from *Carmen*.

Carmen had been given in Minneapolis, and Pat and Julia had heard it together. They were enthralled by it but Mr. Ray grew tired of the Toreador song.

"I'll take your beau anytime, Betsy. Silent Dave is good enough for me."

The Okto Deltas had a whirl of parties, all written up in the *Deep Valley Sun*. There was an Okto Delta tree at Alice's, and Betsy acquired a fine supply of neckbows, back combs, pin cushions, hair receivers.

The Okto Deltas and eight boys drove to St. John in the Blue Jay, a big bob sleigh with hay in the bottom. The night was cold, the snowy landscape ghostly, but the stars had a living brightness in the rich purple sky. Betsy sat next to Dave, tucked under a buffalo robe. Sticks of lemon candy, each stuck into half a lemon, were distributed among the riders. They blew horns, sang in harmony, hopped out of the sleigh and ran alongside, throwing snowballs and even washing faces. Sleighbells jingled and the horses' hoofs rang, and there was an oyster stew at the end of their journey.

Next came the Okto Delta progressive dinner. This was for girls only and each course was served in a different home. It was exhilarating to troop from house to house in the biting cold.

They went to Winona's for the appetizer. With the fruit cup each one received a favor. They went to the Rays' for the fish course; to the Kellys' for turkey; to the Mullers' for salad.

For place cards Tib made cartoons of the girls; Betsy was shown in the new red princesse dress and out of her mouth in a balloon came "David Copperfield." At Irma's, where there was black and orange icing on the cakes, the place cards were slams again. "Silence is golden," Betsy's said. After dinner coffee was served at Carney's, along with apples, nuts and candy. Nut meats had been removed from the walnuts and mottoes were sealed inside. Betsy's said:

"Silence is more eloquent than words."

"The boys were almost crazy," Betsy wrote to Herbert, her Confidential Friend, "because they couldn't make out what kind of a party it was, nor whose house it was at, nor anything. Their royal highnesses were offended to think we could have any fun without them."

Perhaps the progressive dinner turned the trick. At any rate the boys decided to get up a fraternity.

They decided at a spirited party attended by the Okto Deltas in the clubhouse above Lloyd's garage. The eight couples played five hundred and the boys cooked supper in chafing-dishes. They became the Omega Deltas. (The girls thought they knew what the name meant.) There was only one fly in the ointment of general rejoicing. Tony refused to join.

"I tell you I don't like the things. They leave too many people out. I know a fellow who was left out at the U, a swell guy, too, and he was cut up about it. Do you know what they call the ones who don't join? 'Barbs,' 'barbarians.'"

Betsy was indignant. "We don't call the girls who aren't Okto Deltas 'barbs,'" she said. But she had a brief unpleasant memory of Hazel Smith at the St. John game. Okto Delta *wasn't* popular in high school, although so many of its members were.

Betsy did not like to recall this conversation, and she didn't like the fact that the fraternity-sorority business would probably force Tony out of the Crowd. Parties from now on would be for the Okto and Omega Deltas, of course. It was too bad of Tony, she thought.

On the last night of vacation Julia's crowd had a dance. Pat had brought along a dress suit and Julia wore black with a bright red rose at the V of the neck. Mr. Ray didn't like it very well; black was considered daring for girls. But Julia looked lovely, her skin transparently white against the dark silk.

They didn't go to Heinz's after the dance but came home, where Betsy's Crowd had just come in from coasting. They all raided the ice box, and Pat sang the Toreador song. (Fortunately Mr. Ray could sleep through anything.) When the gathering broke up the girls went to Betsy's room, which Julia was sharing during Pat's visit.

"Wasn't Pat in glorious voice?" asked Julia, striking a Carmenlike pose before the mirror.

"Glorious! I'm crazy about Pat."

"He wants me to wear his fraternity pin."

"Are you going to?"

"Maybe. It would certainly impress the Epsilon Iotas. Not that they need impressing!" She took her hand off her hip and dropped down on the bed. "What I'd really like," she said earnestly, "is to go to Germany next year with Fraulein von Blatz. She's going back to Berlin and taking a few pupils with her. Wouldn't it be wonderful if I could go?"

"Perhaps Papa would let you."

"I'm not going to ask him. He's said he wants me to go through college and I've agreed to do it. He's even promised to stake me to some study abroad later on, although he doesn't really want me to be an opera singer. Papa's so good to us, Bettina! No, I'll stick to my part of the bargain, but it's hard."

"Don't you like the U?"

"I'd love it except that I want to be a singer and singers ought to start young. As it is, I'm only interested in Epsilon Iota and my lessons from Fraulein."

"And Pat," teased Betsy.

"Patrick McFadden, certainly," answered Julia,

and started to take down her hair.

"What do you think of Dave?" Betsy asked.

"Oh, I adore that strong silent type. I could be crazy about him, Bettina, if he weren't yours and so awfully young."

Betsy was rapturous. "Really? Maybe I like him better than think I do. He *is* sort of fascinating. You don't know what goes on behind that sober face."

"I'd find out," said Julia, and began to hum an aria from *Carmen*, the one Carmen sings when she comes down from the bridge. Julia sang it under her breath and took the red rose off her dress and threw it at Betsy, just as Carmen tossed it at the hapless Don Jose.

"Oh, Bettina!" she broke off. "You ought to hear *Carmen*. And I ought to be singing it. Of course I'd probably have to be Micaela. That role is better for my voice. She's the girl Carmen takes Don Jose away from, a perfect namby pamby, not at all like me."

Betsy paid no attention.

"The strong silent type," she murmured thoughtfully.

15
O Tempora! O Mores!

THE STRONG SILENT TYPE, Betsy soon discovered, had drawbacks as well as charms. Dave Hunt was handsome, he was fascinating, and she was proud to be his girl. But he could be exasperating! She realized it as the date approached for the Inter-Society debate.

This was late in January, for after vacation came mid-year exams. All activities were suspended during their grim reign.

"*O tempora! O mores!*" groaned Betsy and Tacy, taking Cicero's classic cry for their own. Tib, although German was her language, seized upon it too. She even added to it: "*O tempora! O mores! O Himmel!*"

Alone, in groups, at school, at home, everyone studied. They chanted dates and botanical terms. They heard one another recite poetry which must be memorized.

"'Whan that Aprille with his shoures soote. . . .'"

"I wish that April with his shoures soote was here right now," Cab exclaimed. "Gosh, I hate this English stuff! Do you suppose they have it at the U?"

"Four years of it."

"Not in the engineering course, I'll bet. That's what I'm going to take. Engineers don't give a darn if the Ides of March are percèd to the roote. . . ."

"Not 'ides,' Cab! That's Shakespeare. This is Chaucer."

"Cheer up!" Tacy always said. "Maybe the school will burn down."

It didn't, and they passed in everything, although Betsy's grades weren't what she had planned on Murmuring Lake: Botany, 83; Domestic Science, 84, Cicero, 87, U. S. History, 90, Foundations of English Literature, 93. She rejoiced, nevertheless, and was in a mood for relaxation when word spread that there was to be a party after the Inter-Society Debate, refreshments and games in the Domestic Science room. Boys were asking girls.

Betsy waited, confident of an invitation. Was she not, this year, a "popular" girl? The other Okto Deltas were invited one by one, but nobody invited Betsy. Her confidence waned and her fears grew. She confided in Tib. Tib confided in Dennie who said in a tone of surprise, "Why, Dave is taking Betsy."

Betsy didn't believe it, and steeled herself to go alone. As a loyal Zet, she couldn't stay away. Besides, Hazel Smith was on the team and Betsy wanted to hear her. She was said to be the best girl debater in the state. When the night came Betsy dressed with palpitating care, and Dave arrived on time, serene and silent. The evening was saved for Betsy, although the Philos won the cup.

Soon after this an Okto-Omega party was planned, to be held in the "frat house" above Lloyd's garage. Lloyd promptly invited Tib and Al invited Carney. When Cab invited Irma, Betsy began to grow nervous. Again Tib made inquiries, from Lloyd this time.

She and Betsy planned out beforehand just what she was to say.

"You can call for me at Betsy's. We'll be going together, I suppose. By the way, who's taking Betsy?"

"Dave, of course," Lloyd replied.

Tib hastened to deliver this reassuring news, and during the next few days Betsy flung herself at Dave. She stopped him in the hall and after classes. She manoeuvred to stand beside him in the Social Room. He didn't speak, and she was in a desperate state when Tib arrived to dress with her for the party.

"I'll do your hair in puffs," Tib offered as a gesture of comfort. Puffs were new, and Betsy had not learned to make them. Tib covered Betsy's head with an airy regiment of puffs but Betsy stared in the mirror glumly.

"If he doesn't come I'll stay home."

"You'll do no such thing. You'll go with Lloyd and me."

"I won't. I'll stay home."

"And waste these magnificent puffs?"

Mrs. Ray poked her head in. "He'll show up."

"He'll show up," Margaret echoed gleefully.

Promptly at eight the doorbell rang. Anna shouted with a note of triumph, "Bet-see!" Betsy ran downstairs and there was Dave, with his hair brushed to a shine, a new bow tie and a pleased glow on his face.

"The strong silent type!" Betsy raged. She wished she could hurl it reproachfully at Julia, but Julia had gone back to the U where she had been asked to sing the role of Yum Yum in *The Mikado*. She was rehearsing daily and wrote of little else.

"I won't put up with it!" Betsy stormed later to Tib. "I just won't stand it!"

But she did.

The new term brought basketball contests with all the neighboring towns. Who could resist a proprietary stake in the star of the team? Dave could not take her to the games, of course; she went with Tib and her escort, but everybody knew that Dave would join them afterwards. She watched his long legs scissoring and leaping and heard the adoring roar:

> *"What's the matter with Hunt?*
> *He's all right!"*

Betsy thought basketball more thrilling even than football and talked knowingly of "those rough Spaulding rules."

Honeymoon Trail came to the Opera House, and she heard from Tib that Lloyd and Dave were taking them. It proved to be true. They sat in the parquet, and Betsy had the same uncanny feeling of being grown-up she had when she and Tacy and Tib drank their coffee at Heinz's. It couldn't be, she thought unbelievingly, that they were sitting in the Opera House at night, downstairs, with boys who had paid for their tickets! But they were.

> *"Old, old is honeymoon trail. . . ."*

That was the hit song of the show. Betsy bought it and picked out the chords on the piano when she was alone. She found she could almost play it, which gave a tremendous impetus to her piano lessons and to the hour of practise she split into two parts and found time for every day.

January had been mild, but February came in cold and snowy. The air was filled continually with a white descending haze. Drifts climbed to the window ledges. The thermometer dropped to twenty, thirty, thirty-five below. Tacy and Tib, stopping to call for Betsy in the morning, wore scarves over their faces.

Tib came early so that she could do Betsy's hair. Mr. and Mrs. Ray both protested the practise.

"Betsy doesn't need puffs for school."

"But I'm coming right past the house, Mrs. Ray. I always stop anyway; and I love to do them."

She continued to come, and although Betsy felt a little silly she delighted in the puffs. Sustained by them she joined Tacy in singing the "Cat Duet" at Zetamathian Rhetoricals. It was definitely childish but it had to be sung; it had become a tradition in the Deep Valley High. Betsy read an original poem for rhetoricals. It was named "Those Eyes" and sounded a little like Poe. She wrote more poems than stories on Uncle Keith's trunk this year—when she found time to write at all. This was usually late at night, when she had finished her homework or come in from a party. The house would be quiet; cold, too, sometimes, but she put on a warm bathrobe. She curled up beside the trunk and read poetry and wrote it, and she had an uncanny feeling then, too. This wasn't Betsy Ray, the "popular" girl. This wasn't Betsy Ray, the Okto Delta.

The Sistren still met regularly, sometimes with boys, sometimes alone. The girls brought their sewing to the afternoon parties, and Betsy always brought the jabot. She offered to read aloud if someone would work on it for her and the famous piece of neckwear passed from hand to hand.

"What a souvenir for college!" Carney said. "Samples of everybody's sewing, as well as all these choice knots and spots."

"Those spots you refer to so lightly," said Betsy, "are where I was pricked by a needle. You're taking my heart's blood to Vassar."

Carney was looking ahead to the Vassar entrance exams and working harder all the time. Tacy was sobered by a growing interest in music, but Betsy and Tib continued irrepressible.

Madame DuBarry and Madame Pompadour revived their soirees. These were hilarious affairs, for Cab and Dennie were irrepressible, too. Fast friends, the same age and about the same height, they were a carefree pair. They were, Betsy admitted, more fun than Dave.

But he was fun, too, on outdoor excursions. Groups of four, six, eight Okto and Omega Deltas often braved the cold for moonlight strolls. One night for a lark boys and girls exchanged wraps. Dave was as comical as Dennie, parading in Betsy's furs. He was always the first to sight a pan of fudge set to cool on a doorstep—lawful booty, whether the doorstep belonged to friend or stranger.

In recompense for stolen fudge, perhaps, the groups went serenading. They sang in parts underneath lighted windows, their breath congealing into silver notes.

> "Old, old is honeymoon trail. . . ."
> "You are my rose of Mexico. . . ."
> "My wild Irish rose. . . ."

The Crowd, Julia often said, sang like a trained chorus. But the Okto and Omega Deltas were not quite the Crowd. They missed Tony's rolling bass.

As Betsy had feared, they saw Tony less and less. He still came to the Rays' now and then but he had dropped the Crowd and what he had put in its place was not good. He skipped school, hung around a pool hall which had a bad reputation in Deep Valley. He went with that fast clique of older boys he had been drifting toward early in the winter. Tony had always had a zest for new experiences whether good or bad. But he had been restrained before by his scornful, indulgent, deeply loyal fondness for the Crowd.

Betsy felt pricked all the time by worry about Tony. She wouldn't give in to it; she was having too much fun. But she looked for a chance to say a restraining word and one Sunday night she thought she saw it.

Sometime before she had revived her last year's successful experiment in "reforming." Phil's pipe still hung beside her dressing table. She discovered that Dave had a pipe and secured it to hang beside Phil's. Dennie gave her a sack of tobacco and some cigarette papers. Cab contributed a cigar.

Betsy had protested that. "You don't smoke! You're giving me one of your father's cigars."

"Well, gosh, Betsy!" Cab grinned. "If everyone else is going to be reformed, I want to be reformed, too."

Her father teased her about this enterprise and he brought up the subject as Tony and Betsy stood out in the kitchen watching him make his inimitable sandwiches. He always sat down to make them for he was growing heavier and his feet tired easily. There was often an admiring circle around his chair.

"Have you heard about Betsy turning Carrie Nation?" he asked, spreading slices of bread with butter which he had set out to soften earlier. A cold loin of pork and a jar of mustard stood alongside. "I can't make out why she doesn't object to my cigars."

"You're too old to reform," said Betsy, smoothing his silky dark hair.

Tony searched through his pockets and found a piece of billiard chalk.

"Here," he said. "Add this to your collection. You ought to try to keep boys away from the pool hall, Betsy. It's a den of iniquity, Miss Bangeter says."

Betsy said she would tie the chalk on a ribbon and hang it over her mirror. She laughed into Tony's black eyes which looked hurt, although he was smiling. A new group of guests came to watch Mr. Ray and Betsy went back to the fire. Tony followed with his lazy saunter.

They sat down and looked into the flames, and Betsy said, imitating a grave tone of Julia's, "There was truth in what Miss Bangeter said about that pool hall, Tony. I wish you'd spend less time there and more time—well, at the Rays', or out serenading with the Crowd."

"What Crowd?" asked Tony. His face looked a little bitter. "There isn't any Crowd any more, just a couple of frats. I'm a barb. You don't want me around."

"Tony!" said Betsy. "Don't be ridiculous!"

"Ridiculous, am I?"

"Everybody misses you. The Crowd, Papa, Mamma, Margaret."

"You said one true thing. Margaret does." Tony called out to Margaret, who was reading the funny papers in her father's big chair. "Margaret, I'll beat you a game of parchesi."

Margaret's face lighted and she ran to get the board. Betsy felt snubbed.

Dave came in just then, followed shortly by Squirrelly, and Tib, and Winona. Winona went to the piano and when the parchesi game ended Tony lifted his voice in song. But after the sandwiches were eaten he quickly said good-by.

He shrugged into his overcoat, set his cap at a rakish angle on his bushy curly hair.

"I'll see you when I need some more reforming," he said to Betsy and went out.

16
Margaret's Party

MRS. RAY GAVE A SERIES of three parties on three successive days. It was a common practice to give parties by threes, and practical as well. The same flowers could be used; the chicken salad could be made in bulk; above all the house needed to be disturbed only once. It was certainly disturbed. For three days the Rays ate in the kitchen. Anna was cross, Mr. Ray was moody, Mrs. Ray was glowing and abstracted, and the girls bursting with excitement.

Margaret, excused from school early, ushered the guests upstairs and showed them where to lay their wraps. She wore her party dress, a soft blue silk with invisible stripes, piped in pink. Stiff pink hair ribbons stood out on either side of her small, intent face.

Betsy, Tacy and Tib hurried in after school to put on their party dresses and serve. Balancing plates full of chicken salad, hot rolls, World's Fair pickles and coffee, and second plates with ice cream and angel food cake, they nevertheless found time to smile at the mothers of their friends. Boys' mothers were particularly fascinating.

On the first day Mrs. Ray entertained the church ladies and the wives of her husband's business friends. On the second day Deep Valley's fashionable and wealthy drove to her door. For these two parties her closest friends assisted merely, "assisted throughout the rooms," according to the *Deep Valley Sun*. Such intimates—the High Fly Whist Club crowd, the neighbors—came to the third party which was a more relaxed affair than the two preceding. It simmered down to a chosen few who 'phoned for their husbands and stayed to supper, eating up the last of the food and thoroughly discussing all three events.

They were still busy with this when Betsy went

up to do homework. Margaret had already gone to bed but she called out, "Come here, Betsy," and Betsy went into her room.

It was a small room at the end of the hall. It didn't look like a child's room somehow, in spite of a doll bed with a doll tucked in for the night. It looked like Margaret, neat, grave, full of quiet resources.

The bureau was very precisely arranged, with the pincushion Tony had brought her from Chicago in the center. There was a low rocker where Washington loved to sleep, a low well-ordered bookcase, a sewing basket Mrs. Wheat had given her for Christmas. Framed photographs of members of her family, a Perry print of the Stuart Baby and a colored picture of a collie dog were symmetrically spaced on the walls. Everything was so fastidiously neat that Betsy was surprised to see a doll dress hanging on the bedpost.

She started to remove it but Margaret said, "No. Leave it there."

"Does it belong here?"

"You and Julia keep something hanging on your beds," said Margaret, referring, of course, to the combing jackets.

Betsy, sitting down beside her, took care not to smile. Margaret didn't like being smiled at.

She was sitting up in bed wearing a warm flannel night gown. Without hair ribbons, her braids betrayed their brevity but they were glossy and her face was freshly scrubbed. As always when looking at her younger sister, Betsy admired the long dark lashes. They emphasized the beauty of her wide shining eyes.

"I've been thinking," Margaret said, "that I'd like to give a party."

"Why, that's fine!" Betsy replied. "Mamma is always trying to make you give a party." Which was true. Margaret did not care much for juvenile festivities, nor for children her own age. Urged by Mrs. Ray, they came to play now and then, and Margaret treated them with scrupulous politeness, but she greatly preferred the company of a book, or Washington and Abie.

"Mamma will be delighted," Betsy said. "Who shall we ask?"

"That's just it," Margaret cried. "I don't want to invite a lot of children. I've been lying here thinking about it, Betsy."

She sat up very straight and her eyes glowed.

"You see, Washington and Abie are named for George Washington and Abraham Lincoln, and they have their birthdays this month. So I'd like to give a party for Washington and Abie. I don't want a lot of people. I'd like to have just you and me give a party for Washington and Abie."

Betsy was touched and complimented.

"Why, that's a fine plan! When shall we have it?"

"Lincoln's birthday or Washington's birthday?"

"Maybe it would be safer to pick a day in between. Then neither one's feelings would be hurt."

"That's right. We'll pick a day right in the middle."

"Say, the eighteenth. I think that's Thursday. It's just as well to have it on a Thursday. Anna won't be around to mind our messing up the kitchen."

Betsy leaned back and began to plan. And Margaret hugged her knees in delight, for Betsy knew how to make beautiful plans. She always had and she told them as though she were telling a story.

"We'll have place cards," she said, "like we have at the Okto Delta parties. You and I will make them. We'll draw pictures of cats and dogs or we can cut them out of magazines and paste them on cards."

"I like to paste," said Margaret.

"We mustn't let Abie and Washington see us making them, though."

"Mustn't we?"

"No. We want them for a surprise. And when the day comes we'll brush Washington and Abie and tie ribbons into their collars."

"Washington looks best in pink and Abie in blue. . . ."

"What shall we give them to eat?"

"Something you've learned to make in your Domestic Science class."

"Creamed salmon on toast," said Betsy. She got up and kissed Margaret goodnight. "Go to sleep now, baby. We'll talk about it in the morning."

Margaret snuggled down with an ecstatic sigh.

"Oh, Betsy! It's going to be such fun."

They talked about it the next day and the next, but then came a diversion. Julia's letters about *The Mikado* had grown more and more feverishly excited, and Mr. Ray decided to send Mrs. Ray up to the Cities for the event.

"Julia would probably like her Mamma around to tie her sash and paint her face," he said. "It's a pretty big thing for a freshman girl to have the leading part in an opera."

Mrs. Ray thought so, too, and was very glad to go. In fact, she couldn't imagine Julia getting through it without her. Anna said she could run the house alone and the girls urged their mother to go.

"Now watch out for Margaret!" Mrs. Ray said to Betsy and went off on the four-forty-five. Her letters were even more feverish than Julia's, raving not only about *The Mikado* but also about sorority affairs.

Sororities were still not allowed to rush the freshmen much. Parties were reserved for the now impending Rush Week, which would lead up to Pledge Day and the Great Decision. There was no rule, however, against rushing mothers and the Epsilon Iotas, the Alpha Betas, the Pi Pi Gammas and the rest were certainly rushing Mrs. Ray. They were taking her to matinees, to teas, to luncheons, and Mrs. Ray knew, she wrote, why they were so nice to her. It was because Julia, a freshman, had been chosen to sing Yum Yum. And she was the most adorable Yum Yum!

Mr. Ray chuckled when he read the letters.

"Jule thinks we have a wonderful child."

"You think so yourself," Betsy retorted.

"We know darn well we have three of them," said Mr. Ray. "I'm certainly glad I made Jule go. She's having a big time."

Betsy enjoyed being lady of the house, planning meals, tying Margaret's hair ribbons. She brought friends in every day after school and she and Margaret didn't get around to making place cards. Betsy wasn't too troubled by this. She was accustomed to making extravagant plans which she didn't carry out. Margaret mentioned the party just once, as Betsy was hurrying off to school one morning.

"Shall I tell Washington and Abie about—you know what?"

"Oh, yes. Invite them."

"Will it be on Thursday?"

"Probably. After school."

Thursday noon Anna said, "I'll be gone when you get home from school, lovey. I'll have everything ready for supper, though."

"You don't need to," said Betsy. "I'll make a Domestic Science supper."

"Well, I hope it turns out," said Anna who didn't think too highly of Domestic Science since a recent day when cream puffs, tried at home, had failed lament-ably to live up to their name.

"Be a good girl if you get in ahead of me," Betsy said to Margaret. Margaret smiled; she didn't speak. The party for Washington and Abie was still a secret between them.

Betsy fully intended to come home promptly but a succession of things interfered. Tib had to stay after school for make-up work and persuaded Betsy to wait for her.

"I won't be two minutes."

Cab and Dennie, as it happened, waited too, and when Tib came out of German class after not two minutes but ten, they proposed going to Heinz's for peach pecan sundaes.

"I have to go home," Betsy objected.

"Fine," said Cab. "Go home by way of Heinz's."

"We'll hurry," Tib promised.

And they hurried going down but coming home they loitered, acting silly, trying to walk on snow drifts which capsized under their weight. Tib and Dennie left them at the corner of Plum Street and Broad and climbing the hill with Cab Betsy realized suddenly how late it had grown. The sun was so low that the glow had gone off the snow. It went off her spirits, too.

"Oh, we can have a party for the animals anytime! It doesn't need to be this particular day," she thought, but she quickened her steps, and after she had parted from Cab she went still faster. Feeling guilty she sang and made a lively racket as she ran up the porch steps.

It seemed odd that no lights shone through the windows. Margaret knew how to light the gas. Going quickly into the dim hall, Betsy saw that preparations had been made for the party in the parlor. Four sofa cushions had been laid around a luncheon cloth spread on the floor. A magazine lay open with a paste pot and a pair of scissors near. Margaret must have started to make the place cards. But where were they? Where was Margaret?

Betsy went into the shadowy kitchen. She saw an empty salmon can, and the door of the oven stood open. Had Margaret been making toast to go with the salmon? Then where was it? Where was Margaret?

"She's gone over to see Mrs. Wheat," thought Betsy. But she knew she didn't believe it. If she believed that Margaret was cozily drinking cambric tea next door, she wouldn't have this queer feeling in her stomach.

Washington didn't look up from the couch where he was sleeping, but Abie had come to meet her and now brushed against her ankles.

"Where's Margaret?" Betsy asked him.

Abie barked, a sharp bark and was silent.

Betsy went to the foot of the stairs and called, "Margaret, where are you?"

She was relieved beyond all reason when Margaret's voice answered, "Here I am. Oh, Betsy, I'm so glad you've come!"

Margaret came running down the stairs. She was wearing her party dress, the blue silk piped with pink she had worn for her mother's parties. Her pink party hair ribbons were tied into awkward bows. One had a small loop and a long end; the other had a big loop and a short end. Betsy felt a pang at her heart when she saw those bows.

"I'm so sorry," she began. "I was slow getting home but we'll have the party tomorrow—"

Margaret interrupted.

"Betsy," she said. "Look at my eye lashes. Aren't they curly?"

"Why, baby, your eye lashes are always curly." But Betsy looked closely at Margaret's beautiful eyes. She drew her to a window and stared intently in the fading light. Margaret's eye lashes had been unusually long. They were short now and the ends were frizzled.

"Margaret!" cried Betsy. "What have you done?"

"I was trying to have the party," Margaret said. "You see, Betsy, Washington and Abie had been invited. I couldn't not have a party after they were invited. I started to make the place cards, but they kept looking and you'd said they weren't supposed to see and I was lonesome if I kept them shut up in my room. So I thought I'd let the place cards go and start the lunch.

"I thought I didn't really need to cream the salmon. They like it just as well the way it comes out of the can. But I wanted to put it on toast to make it a party. So I lighted the oven and it exploded."

"Exploded!" Betsy cried. "What do you mean?"

"It just exploded. There was a big bang. And it made my eye lashes curly."

"What did you do?"

"I turned it off," said Margaret. "Oh, Betsy, I was scared, though! I was awfully scared!" and throwing her arms around her sister Margaret began to cry. She cried in big wrenching sobs which tore at Betsy's heart. Margaret didn't cry often. She was the reserved one, the Persian Princess, she was very different from most girls' little sisters and brothers who were always crying.

Betsy felt a wave of awfulness. She hugged Margaret tight.

"Margaret," she said, forcing her voice to be steady. "Do your eyes hurt? Do they feel funny?"

It seemed to her that a century passed before Margaret answered.

"My eyes are all right. It's just that the lashes are curly. I'd like them that way if I hadn't been so scared . . ." and Margaret began to cry again.

Betsy knew that Margaret wasn't crying only because of her fright. It was her disappointment about the party, the long hours of watching for Betsy who didn't come. Betsy started to cry, too, from relief that Margaret's eyes were safe and because she was sorry and ashamed. But she cried for only a minute. It came to her suddenly that she was sixteen years old, too old to cry in a situation like this where there was something else to do.

She pushed the loose hair back from Margaret's wet cheeks and kissed her.

"We must light the gas and get busy," she said briskly. "Papa will be coming in and I've promised him a Dom. Sci. supper. It was horrid of me to forget the party, but I'm going to try to make it up to Washington and Abie. I'm going to let them sit at the table tonight, right beside us, on chairs. We'll have creamed salmon, of course. And Margaret, I'll tell you what we'll do."

"What?" asked Margaret, drying her eyes and blowing her nose.

"I'm going to bake them a joint birthday cake."

"What does 'joint' mean?"

"It means it will belong to them together. Half will be for Washington and half for Abie. I'll frost half in vanilla and half in chocolate. Come on now."

"We'll give Washington the chocolate side because he's the oldest," Margaret said.

Betsy had learned how to bake cake in her Domestic Science class. She baked a pretty good one. Supper was late but Mr. Ray didn't mind when he heard it was a birthday party. Betsy told him about the oven and he looked at Margaret's eyes keenly but he didn't ask how Margaret had happened to be lighting the oven alone. Perhaps he noticed that Betsy's eyes were red.

When Betsy said her prayers that night she started to cry again.

"Dear God!" she said. "It was good of you not to let anything happen to Margaret's eyes. And this is the year I made the resolution to be better around home. I was going to try to take Julia's place. . . ."

She hadn't, she thought, her conscience aching, done very well at that.

Julia had always been such a wonderful older sister. "Even if I tried, I couldn't be to Margaret what Julia has been to me. There's too much difference in our ages. Six whole years."

It must be lonely, she thought, not to have a sister nearer your age than that.

"I'm going to do the best I can," she promised God, "to keep close to Margaret. I'll never, never, never neglect her again."

She stayed on her knees a long time, her head buried in her arm, thinking about Margaret's frizzled lashes.

What if her mother had come home from the Twin Cities to find that something had happened to Margaret's beautiful eyes?

17

A Bolt from the Blue

MRS. RAY CAME home wearing a new spring hat, bearing gifts and radiant with pride. *The Mikado* had been a glorious success and Julia, an enchanting Yum Yum.

"Even the Twin City papers raved, Bob. Oh, I wish you could have been there! Five sororities sent her flowers. She carried those from the Epsilon Iotas."

"Is that the bunch she's going to join?"

"Yes. She's practically an Epsilon Iota now. They

can't bid her until Pledge Day, though." Mrs. Ray outlined briefly what they all knew already. Pledge Day came at the end of Rush Week. On the evening preceding, all the sororities gave formal dinners to which they invited only the freshmen they definitely planned to bid.

"And the freshman goes to the dinner of the group she plans to accept. Julia will go to the Epsilon Iota dinner. We bought her gown while I was in the cities, Betsy. Yellow satin with a train. It's stunning."

"What do you think of sororities anyway?" Mr. Ray asked in a grumpy tone.

Mrs. Ray hesitated. "Why, the Epsilon Iotas are charming girls. They were lovely to me. But I don't know. . . ."

"What is it?" Mr. Ray wanted to know.

"Well, they're so terribly important to Julia. I don't think it would be that way if she cared more about her University work. But she doesn't, Bob. She really doesn't give a snap about any of her studies except singing. What makes it so bad is that Fraulein von Blatz is going away next year."

Mr. Ray sat silent, troubled.

"I wish she could go to Germany with Fraulein," Mrs. Ray said.

Mr. Ray was silent a long time, and Mrs. Ray, Betsy and Margaret watched him while he puffed on his cigar, blowing thoughtful rings.

"No, Jule," he said at last. "I think I'm doing the right thing in asking her to go through the U. Music is a very hard career. She's too young to make such an important decision.

"I've told her she can do as she pleases after she's through college. I'll even scrape up the money to help her. But I'm hoping that she'll meet someone she wants to marry, settle down and use her voice for lullabies," said Mr. Ray looking pleased.

Betsy thought that he didn't entirely understand Julia. No matter whether she went through the University or not, Julia would give her life to music. But Betsy didn't speak, for like all the family she had a profound respect for her father's wisdom. She was even willing to concede that the experiment of college was a wise one. He wanted Julia to be sure, just as he had wanted Julia and Betsy to be sure before they joined the Episcopal Church.

Lent had begun and Betsy, Tacy and Tib had all given up dancing. Betsy was glad to make a sacrifice, for worry about Tony and repentance about Margaret weighed her down a little.

"Now," she wrote to Herbert, "will I show an unparalleled exhibition of courage, steadfastness, self-denial, etc.!!!!!!"

She did shortly, for she refused to go with Dave to

the basketball dance. (Not that he asked her; she refused him in advance, via Tib and Lloyd.)

Mrs. Ray had brought her the *Soul Kiss* music from the cities. Betsy found, to her delight, that she could play the waltz. Tony, Cab, Tacy and Tib sang it to her stumbling accompaniment—when Winona wasn't around, and they couldn't do better.

Miss Mix was making Betsy a new dress for Easter. Shadow rose, with a high waistline, long tight satin sleeves and a directoire sash, also of satin, knotted low on the left side. She and her mother bought her a black chopping-bowl hat trimmed with the same shade of rose.

The snow was melting and it was fun to walk after school with the sun on one's head and slush under foot. Robins and bluebirds sang in the bare trees and there were pussy willows and red-winged blackbirds in the slough.

Cars which had been put away through February were appearing in the muddy streets. Phyllis Brandish again drove Joe Willard down to the *Sun* after school. The Okto Deltas would have enjoyed rattling about in Carney's auto but Carney was working too hard for that. She was buckling down to study on those college entrance exams.

The juniors, too, were looking ahead. Every year they entertained the seniors at a banquet, which was the outstanding social event of the spring. One of

Betsy's wishes, when she made her plans on Murmuring Lake, had been to head up a committee for the junior-senior banquet.

"Do you know what committee I'd like to have?" she asked Tacy, walking to school on the day of the class meeting to discuss the banquet. "The decorating committee. That sounds queer, I know, because I'm not a bit artistic, but I have an idea I'd like to carry out."

"What is it?" Tacy asked.

"Turn the school into a park for banquet night. Move in potted palms, and some porch swings. Make the tables in the Dom. Sci. room look like picnic tables. Have a fish pond—we could fish for packages in it. And maybe a Lovers' Lane."

"Why, Betsy!" Tacy cried. "That's a wonderful idea."

"Oh, I hope I can do it!" Betsy cried. "I'm apt to be head of some committee, so why can't it be the decorating committee?"

The meeting took place after school and the Okto Delta juniors sat together. They had become more and more clannish since resentment at the sorority had begun to seep through the school. Betsy would have been with them but she sat on the platform with the other class officers. Stan Moore was president as he had been the year before. He and Betsy had both kept their offices and Betsy, secretly, hoped to be re-elected for the senior year.

Stan, a tall relaxed boy, usually conducted a meeting admirably but today he acted nervous. After rambling on about the banquet, stressing its importance, of which everybody was aware, and announcing the date in May which had already been fixed, he said that he was ready to name the committee heads.

"Oh, dear!" thought Betsy. "I hope I get the decorating committee."

Stan cleared his throat and started to read. He stopped and cleared it again but then he continued in a bold voice. It was a surprising list. The six Okto Delta juniors were all prominent in school, especially Betsy, Alice and Winona. But not one was named for any committee. The decorating committee went to Hazel Smith.

The Okto Deltas sat very still when Stan had finished. Betsy, on the platform, swallowed hard. When the discussion passed to other matters, they stole furtive looks at one another, but even Winona was silent.

At the end of the meeting Hazel hurried over to Betsy.

"I want to get you before somebody else does," she said. "Will you serve on my committee? Where's Tacy? I want her, too."

"There she is," said Betsy. "And thank you, Hazel! I'd love to be on your committee."

The class filed out of the assembly room. Carney, waiting in the hall, was puzzled by the dazed expression on the faces of her Okto Delta sisters.

"What's the matter?" she asked.

"We don't know," said Winona. "Maybe we all have poison ivy."

"Why do you say that?"

"Not one of us was given a committee."

"That's funny," Carney said. "I wasn't given a senior committee either. I thought perhaps it was because I was studying so hard." But that, everyone knew, was unlikely. Carney had always been outstanding in her class. "It looks as though they had something against us as a group," she added, looking sober.

"Can it be dear old Okto Delta?" asked Winona.

"I've heard," Alice said, "that we're called a bunch of snobs."

"That isn't fair," cried Betsy. "We're not the least bit snobbish."

"And we can live without their old committees," said Tib, tossing a yellow head.

But Betsy's mind flashed ahead to next year, her senior year, her last in Deep Valley High. She wouldn't, she admitted, like it at all not to have a share in next year's thrilling climactic activities.

The Okto Deltas ignored the whole matter at their next meeting, a particularly silly one.

"The Sistren," Secretary Ray wrote in the minutes,

"played statues, leadman, and other kid games. They acted dippy."

The girls tried to gloss over their unfortunate position in school, but they felt a little subdued and most of them applied themselves energetically to school work.

Betsy had had a good year in English. Her work had been merely acceptable in other classes; she and Tacy and Tib had not yet made their herbariums for Botany. But ever since Miss Fowler had praised her work last November Betsy had worked hard on Foundations of English Literature.

She always looked forward to English class, both because she liked the subject and because she enjoyed the competition of Joe Willard. They never saw each other outside of school but in English class there was a bond between them. They talked for each other's benefit sometimes; they sought each other's eyes when a good point was made; they smiled across the room when something funny happened. This intimacy always stopped at the door of the classroom and Betsy was surprised one March day to find him waiting for her.

His hands were in his pockets and he was smiling, his eyes very bright under the light crest of hair.

"Hey!" he said. "What do you think of the topic for the Essay Contest?"

"Why . . ." said Betsy. "I haven't heard what it is."

"You haven't? Well, it's a queer one: 'The History of the Deep Valley Region.'"

"'The History. . . .'" Betsy's face lighted with a smile of utter joy. She rose on her toes. "Joe Willard!" she cried, shaking her finger in his face. "You haven't a chance!"

"Oh, is that so!"

"Yes, it's so! Were you even born in Deep Valley?"

"I was born in Brainerd. But you didn't start taking notes on local history in the cradle, did you?"

"Practically," said Betsy. "You see, my father loves it. His people came to Iowa in a covered wagon and he was only nineteen when he struck out for himself and came up here. Besides, there's Grandma Slade."

"Grandma Slade?"

"Tom's Grandmother. We always have Thanksgiving dinner with the Slades, and you ought to hear her stories. Why, she was here when the Sioux went on the warpath, blankets, feathers, tomahawks and all."

"Look here!" Joe said, looking at her smilingly. "You mustn't be spilling all your material. I'm your rival, you know. I'm agin you. I'm the fellow the Philomathians picked just on purpose to outwit you."

Betsy's expression changed. She stopped smiling and a quick line of worry appeared between her brows.

"Come to think of it, the Zets haven't picked me. When did you find out that you were chosen?"

"O'Rourke told me this morning."

Her face smoothed out. "Then it's probably all right; Clarke will speak to me after History class."

"You haven't any doubt about being picked, have you?"

"N . . . n . . . no," Betsy answered. "Still . . . I've lost two years running."

"They couldn't put up anybody half as good as you are and you know it," Joe replied.

Betsy smiled at him. "Why, thank you," she said. "I didn't know you had it in you. I never expect bouquets from you, somehow—only brickbats. I'm not really worried about being chosen. Just the same, you can keep your fingers crossed."

He crossed his fingers, holding them high above his head as Betsy went away.

In History class Betsy looked at Miss Clarke with a certain urgency. It seemed to her, however, that Miss Clarke was avoiding her eyes. She was greatly relieved when, at the end of the period, Miss Clarke said, "Betsy, will you stop in to see me after school?"

Again relief flowed into Betsy's face. Her mouth swept upward in a smile.

"Yes, Miss Clarke. I'd be glad to."

She went out walking on air.

"What are you so happy about?" Tib asked.

"Clarke wants to see me after school. And I think it's the Essay Contest."

"Why, of course, you'll be chosen for that. You

always are," said Tacy. And Tib added, "You know you write better than anyone in school."

"Except Joe," said Betsy, laughing. "And I'm going to give him a run for his money this year. The subject is perfect for me, just perfect. Oh, I'm so happy!"

She was, she realized suddenly, eager to start work on a serious project. She found herself looking ahead to it, almost with longing. She would enjoy it all after her gay winter: the quiet of the library, her friend Miss Sparrow, the long hours of hard work, Joe's stimulating company.

He liked her. She knew he did, Phyllis or no Phyllis. If they were working together again at a little table in back of the stalls, they would get acquainted as she had often wished they could.

"I really want him for a friend," Betsy thought. "Not just that I'm sweet on him. We have so much in common. We were intended to be friends."

At noon she told her family the subject for the Essay Contest.

"Isn't that nifty? Can you imagine anything more perfect?"

"Have you been asked to compete yet?" her father inquired.

"Not yet. But I'm sure I will be."

"Of course, she will," Mrs. Ray said. "Even if the judges went out of their minds last year and the year before."

"They didn't," Betsy said. "Joe Willard can write. But I think I can beat him on Deep Valley history. At least I'll have fun trying."

She went back to school smiling.

But her heart sank, the smile left her face, when she entered the history room after school. For the smile on Miss Clarke's sweet, artless face was forced. She looked unhappy.

"Sit down, Betsy," she said. "I have some bad news for you."

"Bad news?"

"Stan Moore has been chosen to represent the junior Zetamathians on the Essay Contest."

Before she could stop them, tears sprang to Betsy's eyes.

"Oh, no, Miss Clarke!" she cried. "Not this year, when the subject is Deep Valley! I love Deep Valley! I could write about it! I could win!"

She stopped and rubbed the tears savagely out of her eyes.

"What am I saying?" she asked. "You must excuse me, Miss Clarke. Of course, you and Miss Fowler are quite right to try someone else. I've lost two years running."

"Betsy," said Miss Clarke, taking off her glasses and wiping her eyes, "Miss Fowler and I think you could write a better essay than any Zetamathian in the school. Maybe I shouldn't tell you that. But it's true."

"Then why. . . ?" Betsy asked.

"There's a lot of feeling around school," Miss Clarke answered, "that your crowd has everything. You are pretty outstanding, you know. Until recently there wasn't much jealousy. You were all democratic and popular. But this year . . . people don't like the sorority-fraternity business! They just don't like it.

"Zetamathian and Philomathian are school societies. They shouldn't be monopolized by any one crowd. If we gave you a third chance to compete in the Essay Contest, after you lost the first two years, it might add to the hard feeling which has already been built up against your group. You wouldn't like that, would you?" Betsy shook her head, unable to speak.

"If it was anything but Deep Valley history I wouldn't feel so bad," she said at last in a choked voice, and Miss Clarke, who had just replaced her glasses took them off and started rubbing them again.

"Never mind!" said Betsy, rising. "Stan will write a good essay. Good-by, Miss Clarke"—and she darted out.

She went to the cloak room where Tacy was waiting and buried her face in her coat.

Tacy put her arms around her. "You didn't get it?"

Betsy shook her head.

"But how could you help but get it?"

Betsy shook her head even more frantically.

"I don't know what Clarke and Fowler can be

thinking of," said Tacy, hugging her harder. "They must be crazy. It's just throwing the Essay cup away."

Betsy took her face out of the coat. She blew her nose and wiped her eyes and put some face powder on her nose. Hooking on to Tacy's arm, she started talking about something else and they went down the stairs and out of the school.

When she saw Joe Willard next day she was lightly regretful.

"They've given you real competition this year. No one less than the president of the junior class."

His face was swept with amazement and, Betsy realized with doleful satisfaction, disappointment.

"Stan Moore? Why, they must be crazy. Stan's a swell guy but you can write circles around him."

"You shouldn't have written circles around me last year and the year before," she said.

Joe scowled. He stood with his hands in his pockets, his thick light brows drawn together.

"I'll be thinking of you," Betsy said, "slaving down there in the library when the snow melts and the violets come out and the picnicking season begins."

Joe didn't answer. He strode off in the direction of Miss Clarke's room. But Philomathians were allowed no voice in Zetamathian affairs. After a moment Joe came out of Miss Clarke's room still scowling, and Stan Moore began work on the Essay Contest.

18

Two More Bolts from the Blue

ONE APRIL EVENING the Rays sat at supper talking about Julia. Beyond the windows, winter still lingered in a sad, opalescent sky. But the day had been spring-like. Melted snow had been rushing down the gutters in foaming rivers on which Margaret had sailed boats. Betsy had walked to the slough for marigolds. Mr. Ray wore a pansy in his buttonhole, and there was rhubarb short-cake for dessert.

The Rays were talking about Julia because the week ahead was the supreme one to which she had been looking forward. It was nothing less than Rush Week. Luncheons, teas, and masquerades would lead in gay procession up to that formal dinner at the Epsilon Iota house for which she had bought the yellow satin dress.

"How do the freshmen get their bids?" asked Betsy, eating with good appetite.

"Through the mail on Pledge Day morning. Special delivery," Mrs. Ray replied. "In the afternoon they go to the house of their choice to be welcomed and cried over and given a pledge pin. It's very thrilling, the girls say."

"It's tough on the ones who don't get those special delivery letters," Mr. Ray remarked.

"Yes, it is." Mrs. Ray looked distressed. "I'm certainly thankful that Julia is one of the lucky ones."

"Week after next she'll be home for Easter and tell us all about it," Betsy said.

Anna, who was clearing the table, looked out the window. "Why, there's Mr. Thumbler's hack!"

Everyone jumped up and Mr. Ray observed, "It must be Aunt Lucinda."

Aunt Lucinda sometimes came to make a visit uninvited.

"Are there any creamed potatoes left?" Mrs. Ray asked anxiously. "And if you haven't cut the short-cake, Anna, cut it to serve one more."

"The McCloskeys," remarked Anna, "didn't have relatives who came just at mealtime."

Betsy and Margaret couldn't understand her grumpiness. They ran to the window to see Aunt Lucinda getting out of the hack. But to everyone's amazement it was Julia who alighted.

She was wearing her winter hat and coat and the effect was bleak. She looked very small, standing beside the hack in the twilight. Mr. Ray rushed out to pay Mr. Thumbler and Mrs. Ray, Betsy and Margaret followed. With their arms about Julia they ascended the steps, exclaiming joyfully.

Julia smiled and returned their kisses but her face was pale.

"You look sick, darling," Mrs. Ray cried. "Is that why you came home?"

"I'm not sick," answered Julia.

"We thought you were Aunt Lucinda," Margaret said.

"We were awfully surprised to see you, on account of next week being Rush Week."

"And the week after that, your vacation . . ."

"Never mind about all that until she's had some supper," Mr. Ray put in.

"I don't want any supper. I couldn't eat anything, really. I . . . I ate on the train." Julia took off her hat and coat and Margaret ran to hang them up. Julia sat down in the parlor and the Rays gathered about her, anxious now to know what lay behind her white strained face.

She told them at once. "The Epsilon Iotas have dropped me!"

"What?"

"How could they 'drop' you?" Margaret asked, bewildered.

"They're not rushing me any more. I'm not invited to any of the Epsilon Iota parties."

"Why . . . why . . . that's impossible!" Mrs. Ray gasped. "Not even to the formal dinner?"

"Especially not to that."

Everyone thought of the yellow satin dress, but no one mentioned it.

"I've been dropped," Julia repeated, her lips trembling. "I've been tried and found wanting."

"What perfect nonsense!" Mr. Ray interjected, but he, too, looked pale.

"Are the others still rushing you?" Mrs. Ray demanded.

"Yes," said Julia. "But that doesn't interest me. I'm going to be an Epsilon Iota or I won't be anything. I'll be a barb." She shut her lips tight.

The Rays were silent for a moment, stunned. It was incomprehensible. Julia, the beautiful, the talented, their darling . . . dropped! A barb!

"But why? Why? What do they think you've done?" Mrs. Ray cried at last.

"I don't know."

"Can't you ask them?"

"Certainly not! I have to act as though I didn't even notice they had dropped me. Of course, I can't help but notice it. All year the girls have been so lovely to me, and now they treat me almost like a stranger. They speak when we meet, of course. But that's all.

"One of them told me—she wasn't supposed to but she did—that they haven't stopped liking me. They act this way because they know they can't bid me, and it would hurt me more if they rushed me to the very end."

"But why can't they bid you?"

"The vote has to be unanimous, and someone doesn't want me."

"Well, the very idea!" Mrs. Ray cried. "I'd like to burn the University down!"

"I'd like to murder the whole bunch," Betsy exclaimed.

Mr. Ray put his arm around Margaret. "Julia isn't the only little girl whose feelings have been hurt, I imagine," he said. "It's a mighty funny thing that the State University, supported by the public, can have private clubs which are so important."

But Mrs. Ray couldn't think now about the ethics of Greek letter organizations. She was astounded and dismayed.

Julia was treated as though she were sick. She was put to bed and Anna brought up a hot lemonade. Mrs. Ray, Betsy and Margaret sat in her room talking in hushed voices while Mr. Ray tramped the house looking sober and distracted.

"Are you sure, are you sure, you don't want to join one of the others?" Mrs. Ray asked. "The Alpha Betas were very nice, I thought, and so were the Pi Pi Gammas."

"I'm positive," Julia said.

Mrs. Ray kept naming the Epsilon Iotas she had met on her visit. Ann, the dark queenly one; Patty and Joan, the twins; blonde Norma.

"I can't imagine them not being friendly."

"They barely speak to me. But don't you see? That's the kind thing to do. If I've been dropped there's no sense being nice and giving me false hopes."

"Have you any idea which one doesn't want you?"

"None in the world."

Mr. Ray paused in the doorway. "Are you staying home a while?"

"Oh, no!" said Julia. "I'm going back tomorrow night."

"Darling!" cried Mrs. Ray. "I don't think you'd better go back! Why don't you have a sore throat and stay home a little while?" But Julia shook her head.

"No," she said. "I'm going back. But just for today I'll have a sore throat. Oh, it's so good to be home!" She put her arms around Margaret who was sitting on the bed beside her, and buried her face in Margaret's lap.

"It was awful this last week!" she sobbed. "You can't imagine! Those girls I've grown to like so much, hurrying past me, looking the other way. Everyone asking me what sorority I think I'll join and me not joining any unless I can have the one I want."

"Whatever one you joined," said Betsy, choking, "you'd make it the best on the campus just by joining it."

But Julia, without speaking, shook her head.

The next morning early Betsy heard her stirring and went into her room. Julia was dressing.

"I'm going down to early church," she said.

"Mind if I go along?"

"I never mind having you along, Bettina."

They stole out of the house. Yesterday's puddles were frozen but robins were singing and flying about in a dim light. A Persian rug had been unrolled in the sky above the German Catholic College.

Julia and Betsy did not talk much on their way. They went inside the church and dropped to their knees.

The Rev. Mr. Lewis did not seem to notice them. He was always like that at early church.

"Lift up your hearts," he said.

"We lift them up unto the Lord."

"Let us give thanks unto our Lord God."

"It is meet and right so to do."

The altar was snowy and fresh, with candles gleaming, and the service passed like a dream. The Rev. Mr. Lewis said, "The peace of God which passeth all understanding keep your hearts and minds . . ."

Julia stayed on her knees a long time and when she and Betsy emerged at last into the cold and the daylight, peace shone in her face.

She squeezed Betsy's arm. "I'm all right now," she said. "Going to church is a wonderful help. It makes"—she laughed ruefully—"even sororities seem pretty small."

She went on thoughtfully, "I was weak to come home. It's a temptation to come running back to the warmth and tenderness of home when the world is cruel. But I won't be a coward any more. I'll go back to the U and go through Rush Week with my head up, and then I'm going to get down to work. I only wish Fraulein wasn't going away."

"When is she going?" Betsy asked.

"Not till the end of the term. I'm thankful for that.
I have so much to be thankful for, Bettina! My family,
my music, my glorious plans for my life. . . ."

Her face looked exalted, as it looked when she
sang.

The rest were at breakfast when they came in, and
Betsy had the feeling that the topic of conversation
was abruptly changed. She saw her father look
keenly at Julia's face, and later she heard him say to
her mother, "We won't interfere. She has the thing
licked."

During the rest of the day Julia was quite like herself. She praised the Perfection Salad Anna had made
especially for her; she bathed white woolly Abie
because Margaret delighted to assist at this function;
and she sang for all the friends and neighbors who
dropped in.

At Sunday night lunch Katie asked innocently,
"You'll be having fun next week, won't you? Isn't it
Rush Week?"

Betsy's heart melted with pity, but Julia was
serene. "Rush Week doesn't mean anything to me.
The Epsilon Iotas have dropped me. And since they're
the only crowd I care for, I don't think I'll join a
sorority."

"I wouldn't either in that case," Katie said in her sensible way.

A little later Julia drew Betsy aside. "It's surprising how much better I feel since I've said out loud in public that the Epsilon Iotas have dropped me. I dreaded that so, and it wasn't half bad."

She returned to Minneapolis that night, and when the family got back from the train Betsy started upstairs with her school books but her father asked her to wait.

"Your mother and I would like to let you in on something we've been discussing."

Betsy went into the parlor and sat down. He told her the news and it was another bolt from the blue.

Pacing the floor yesterday, he had decided that Julia should go to Germany next year. He had been thinking for some time, he said, that Mrs. Ray was right, that Julia was never going to want anything but opera. Well, if that was the case, she didn't need to stay on at the U and be made unhappy by this sorority business.

He had informed Mrs. Ray who had promptly wept for joy and pleaded with him to tell Julia.

"I was tempted to myself," Mr. Ray admitted, "although I knew it would be wrong. She has to learn to take hard knocks. We can't always take them for her, nor for you and Margaret either, Betsy. I was wavering, and then she came back from church and I could see that she was going to be all right. So we're going to let her go through this darn fool week on her own steam."

"It seems cruel," Mrs. Ray said anxiously. "But Papa thinks it's right."

"I think so, too," said Betsy. "Julia had sort of a . . . triumph . . . today. She would feel cheated if it was all for nothing."

"But, oh, what a week she has ahead of her!" Mrs. Ray cried pityingly. "Those parties! The gossip! Pledge Day morning and not being bid! How can she stand it?"

"She'll stand it like hundreds of other little girls are standing it," said Mr. Ray.

But he looked unhappy, too.

19

Still Another Bolt
from the Blue

THAT WEEK WAS ONE of the longest and hardest the
Ray family had ever known. All of them were suffering with Julia. Betsy and her mother talked of little
else. Margaret made her sister a penwiper. Anna
cleaned Julia's room, shaking the curtains fiercely as
though they were the Epsilon Iotas.

"Whatever *they* are!" Anna muttered.

Mr. Ray tried to cheer himself by planning Julia's

trip to Germany. He said over and over again how sensible they were not to tell her the good news this week, and Mrs. Ray agreed. But on the night of the formal dinners, Mrs. Ray weakened.

"Let's call her up and tell her, Bob. She won't need to tell anyone else."

"All right," said Mr. Ray, yielding suddenly. "She's gone through a tough week. There's no need to make her wear a hair shirt, after all."

Mrs. Ray flew to the telephone and called the dormitory, but Julia was out. She left word for Julia to call back. Julia didn't call, and the morning of Pledge Day Mrs. Ray 'phoned again. Again Julia was out. But she had received the message last night, the matron said.

"She doesn't want to talk to us," Mrs. Ray exclaimed. "She can't bear to. Oh, Bob, we should have told her before she went back!"

"See here!" said Mr. Ray. "All the other little girls who have been dropped by sororities or were never rushed at all haven't got families who are going to send them to Europe. If they can take it, Julia can. If she doesn't want to talk to us, it's because she knows we're a bunch of sissies who would only weaken her courage."

But Mr. Ray went down to the shoe store looking grim.

Julia came home next day, and according to family tradition Mr. Ray should have met her at the train alone, bringing her home to dinner under pledge of not letting her say a word. Today, however, the whole family went to meet her.

"No telling what kind of shape she'll be in. She may want to go right to bed."

"I'll have a hot water bottle ready," said Anna, who was a little vague as to just what kind of calamity overhung Julia.

"I wonder, I wonder whether she'll blame us for not telling her," Mrs. Ray kept saying.

Mr. Ray hitched up Old Mag, and, filled with mingled sympathy and dread, the family drove to the station. The train rushed down the track beside the river to a panting steaming halt and Julia stepped off wearing a radiant smile, a gigantic new spring hat and a corsage bouquet almost as big. She flew at her family kissing and hugging.

"Be careful!" Mrs. Ray cried. "Don't crush your flowers! They're so beautiful."

"Not so beautiful as what's underneath them," said Julia, and right on the station platform she slipped off her coat. On her shirt waist a gold pin was gleaming.

"Look! I'm pledged Epsilon Iota."

"Julia!"

"Were you at the dinner?"

"Was that why you weren't at home when we 'phoned?"

"No," said Julia. "I was walking all that evening. I

walked all the way to downtown Minneapolis and back. I had to keep walking to keep going. I was so unhappy. It was the worst night of my life."

"But then—how do you happen to be wearing the pin?"

"See here!" said Mr. Ray. "We can't go into all this standing up. Pile into the surrey and I'll drive you home."

"I won't stir one foot until we've heard it all," Mrs. Ray replied.

"Then come on in the station and have some coffee," said Mr. Ray, who hated standing on his feet. So over a ring of coffee mugs, with milk for Margaret, Julia told her story.

"Well, I've known all along that one girl was keeping me out." She began to laugh. "Now I know the reason why. I've promised not to tell, so all of you must promise not to tell. It's because of Pat. Norma—the blonde, Bettina—is one of the girls I took Pat away from. *She* was blackballing me.

"The rest of the girls were just crazy to have me, and the more things I did around school—singing in *The Mikado*, acting in plays and so on—the crazier they were. They all knew Norma was voting against me, and they knew the reason why, but there wasn't anything they could do about it. Except to keep on voting over and over again, which they did. But there was always one blackball."

"Really black?" asked Margaret, her eyes enormous.

"Blacker than ink," said Julia. "And the night before Pledge Day they had the formal dinner without me, and I was walking the streets.

"But it seems that alumnae are very important in a sorority. They put up the money for houses and things. And one of the alumnae, who had seen me in *The Mikado*, was determined I was going to be an Epsilon Iota. That night, while I was walking the streets and weeping, she was gathering up a lot of other alumnae and after the banquet they all descended on the Chapter House and said, 'We want Julia Ray! We want Julia Ray!'" Julia chanted as at a football game.

"They called for a ballot and there was still one vote against me. They kept right on voting all night long and poor Norma couldn't hold out. At last, when it was almost morning, everyone was voting yes. So they sent my invitation over by messenger— they had had it all ready, lying on the table. It reached me at the dormitory yesterday morning and I went to the Epsilon Iota house and was pledged right along with the rest."

"Well for Pete's sake!" said Mr. Ray.

"That doesn't sound very . . . idealistic," Betsy remarked. "It isn't a bit the way I imagined sisterhoods were."

"How did you find out all this?" Mrs. Ray asked.

"Oh, I stayed at the house last night," Julia replied. "I slept with Patty and she told me the whole story. Of course, I promised not to tell. So don't you."

"And you don't mind joining now?" asked Betsy.

"Why, no. Everyone except Norma wanted me all along. Even Norma seemed to want me today. She cried when she kissed me good-by. And they sent me these flowers to make up for all I've gone through."

"They ought to have sent some flowers to your mother, too," Mr. Ray observed.

"And to me!" cried Betsy. "And to Margaret! And for that matter to Anna. She has a hot water bottle in your bed."

"A hot water bottle? For heaven's sake, why?" They all began to laugh but it was half crying. They got up and went out to the surrey, Julia with her arm around her mother. They piled in and drove to High Street.

Julia rushed into the house and kissed and hugged Anna and put her bouquet in the ice box and started flinging things about. She sat down at the piano and began to play a new tune.

"I brought you all the *Stubborn Cinderella* music, Bettina."

Mr. Ray didn't go back to the shoe store, and it was like a holiday.

In the evening Tony and Cab and Dennie and Tacy and Katie and Tib came in, and there was more music, and peanut fudge and excitement. Everyone examined Julia's pledge pin and she talked constantly about Epsilon Iota—the house, the girls, plans for the spring formal dance and whether or not she would take Pat.

"I don't think I will," she confided to Betsy, "on account of Norma. After all, she's my sister in Epsilon Iota now."

Usually when young people were rampaging through the house, Mr. and Mrs. Ray went to bed, although Mrs. Ray never went to sleep until the girls came up. Tonight, however, they stayed in the parlor, and when everyone went home about eleven o'clock, Julia and Betsy joined them.

Mr. Ray sat in his big chair, his legs crossed, smoking a cigar. Mrs. Ray, very bright-eyed, sat in her slender rocker. Julia flung herself down on the couch but Betsy stood in the doorway, sensing that her father and mother were now going to make their stupendous announcement.

"Julia," said Mr. Ray, "I want to have a talk with you."

His tone was so serious that Julia sat upright.

"What is it, Papa?"

"It's a talk I might postpone," he went on, "except

for one reason. I suppose there's some expense involved in this Epsilon Iota?"

"Yes, there's an initiation fee. A hundred dollars or so. Are you worried about the money, Papa?"

"Not if you're going back to the University next year. But if you aren't, you may have to make a choice."

"But, of course, I'm going back. I thought that was all settled. I was planning to stay at the U even if the Epsilon Iotas didn't bid me."

"I know," said Mr. Ray. "But your mother and I have been doing a lot of talking. We've made some plans we want to talk over with you. I thought of going into this last week when you were feeling so badly, but it seemed like giving you some help you hadn't asked for and didn't need. It seemed best to let you go through Rush Week on your own steam."

"Which I did," said Julia proudly.

"I was the one who couldn't quite stand it," said Mrs. Ray. "That's why we telephoned you Thursday night. I'm glad now we couldn't get you."

"You know why I didn't call back," said Julia. "I was feeling too badly to talk. The next morning I found out what was in the wind, but I wanted to be sure before I called you, and after that I wanted to surprise you with my pin." She patted it fondly. Then her expression grew serious. "What do you want to talk about, Papa? If you've got any worries I don't need to join Epsilon Iota right now."

Everyone was smiling, but Mr. Ray grew sober. "Julia," he said, "how would you like to go to Germany next year and study with Fraulein von Blatz?"

Julia stared at him. Betsy saw the color drain out of her face.

"I thought," said Julia, "that was out of the question. I thought you felt strongly about my putting that off."

"I did," said Mr. Ray. "But I've come to see that your singing is all you really care for. And Fraulein von Blatz is not only an excellent teacher, Mrs. Poppy says; she's a very fine woman and will have a big class of young Americans living near her in Berlin. It sounds safe enough and your mother and I have to let you go some day. We want you to go now if it's best for you, and I believe it is."

Now Julia was silent, deeply and intensely silent. The parlor quivered with her silence.

"The reason I brought it up now," said Mr. Ray, "is that it has some bearing on your joining Epsilon Iota. Germany would be, Mrs. Poppy tells me, quite an expensive business. You don't just study singing when you go abroad to study singing. You study acting, too, and languages and a lot of other things. I can swing it, but I won't have any money to spare. I wouldn't want you to go to the expense of joining a sorority—"

Julia interrupted. Yet she didn't actually interrupt for she seemed not to have heard the last few things he had said. She got up, still pale, and crossed the room. She put her arms around her father and tears began running down her cheeks.

"But you don't want me to be an opera singer!" she said.

"I never said I didn't."

"You'd rather I just got married. That's why you wanted me to go to the University first."

"I don't want you to be an opera singer unless you're darn' well sure you want to be," said Mr. Ray. "It's a hard life. But your mother has seen all winter that your heart was only in your singing. That's why you went off your nut about the sorority thing. Perhaps you know best about what you ought to do. I'm willing to send you to Germany next year, if you want to go."

Julia finished crying with her head on her father's shoulder, and then she went to her mother and cried, and to Betsy and cried some more, hugging and swinging her around.

"You'll never be sorry!" she said, turning a joyful face to her father. "You'll never be sorry!"

"Julia," said Mrs. Ray. "You haven't answered Papa's question about Epsilon Iota. I'm afraid you're disappointed not to join after being pledged and all. But you'll have to make a choice."

"What choice?" asked Julia. "There isn't any choice. The girls are swell; it was nice of them to ask me. But I don't know what choice you mean."

"Then you're going next fall," began Mrs. Ray, but Mr. Ray interrupted.

"Here's something I haven't told your mother. There's a good chance to send you in June. The Rev. Mr. Lewis is taking a party over for European travel. They will visit London, Rome and Paris and wind up in Germany. He can leave you there when he brings the rest home. How does that sound to you all?"

Julia began to cry again but she dashed the tears away as though she couldn't be bothered with them.

"In June! Papa! I must be dreaming. Oh, dear, I must hurry and give back Pat's fraternity pin."

"But you're not wearing it!" Betsy cried. "Are you crazy? There's nothing but your Epsilon Iota pledge pin on your shirt waist."

"I'm wearing his pin on my corset cover," Julia said. "It's more romantic that way. Oh, dear, dear, dear! I'm so happy!"

"Well, I'll go put the coffee pot on," said Mr. Ray, moving toward the kitchen.

"Is it too late to 'phone Mrs. Poppy? I wonder what roles I'll be singing? She'll start me on Mozart, probably," said Julia, pacing back and forth across the parlor, a smile on her tear-wet face.

20

"Sic Transit Gloria . . ."

BETSY DID SOME THINKING about sororities during
spring vacation. They weren't at all what she had
thought them to be. Julia's experience made them
seem shallow, and the ease with which Julia had
abandoned the idea of joining one had been an eye-
opener, too.

Sisterhoods! That, thought Betsy, was the bunk. You couldn't make sisterhoods with rules and elections. If they meant anything, they had to grow naturally. She thought how she and Tacy had started to be friends when they were five years old. They had added Tib, Alice and Winona; then Carney and Irma. That had been almost a real sisterhood and it could have gone on forever without hurting anybody's feelings. They might have added Hazel Smith this year.

Or perhaps, Betsy thought, she and Hazel might have had a friendship independent of the Crowd. After all, you couldn't go through life rolling your friendships into one gigantic snowball. You wanted different kinds of friendships, with different kinds of people. She might like someone awfully well whom Tacy wouldn't care for at all. You ought not to go through life, even a small section of life like high school or college, with your friendships fenced in by snobbish artificial barriers.

"It would be like living in a pasture when you could have the whole world to roam in," Betsy thought. "I don't believe sororities would appeal very long to anyone with much sense of adventure."

She wondered whether Julia still had her lofty ideas about sororities and tried to question her. But it was hard to bring Julia back to the subject. She had only a short vacation, yet she had plunged into the study of

German. A singer had to know German, of course, especially if she was going to Berlin.

"Why the dickens didn't I take it up long ago? Here we are living in a town that's half German and we study only Latin. We don't see what a wonderful chance we have to learn a living language. One of your best friends is German, Bettina. If you were studying it, you could practise on her and her parents." And that was all Betsy could get out of Julia, who was on her way to take a lesson in German from the Lutheran minister's wife.

School began again and walking back and forth along High Street, where brownish green buds were swelling on the maples and the bushes around the houses were wearing pale green veils, Betsy continued to try to straighten out the matter of sororities. She had prided herself this year on being a "popular" girl. But she had never been less popular. Unpopularity had lost her a junior-senior banquet chairmanship; it had lost her the Essay Contest. If this went on she wouldn't even have a class or Zetamathian office next year. Yet the school and the school societies, she realized now, were more important to her than Okto Delta.

Of course, the "popularity" with boys had been nice but she wouldn't need to lose that if they gave up Okto Delta. In fact, the boy situation might even be improved by the collapse of the two fraternal organizations.

"Do you know," Winona said, one evening in late April when the Okto Deltas were gathered to celebrate Betsy's seventeenth birthday, "when we talked the boys into getting up that fraternity we should have made them put into their vows that they wouldn't take out any girls but us."

Everyone laughed and someone asked why.

"Because they're straying, that's why. They've almost all got crushes on freshmen girls. Do you feel perfectly sure of Dave?" she asked, looking fixedly at Betsy.

"I haven't seen him for a week," said Betsy.

"Do you know what Squirrelly said to me the other day? 'You Okto Deltas wouldn't mind, would you, if we boys brought some other girls to the parties?'"

"He didn't!"

"The nerve of him!"

"I got so mad I gave him his Omega Delta pin back, and it wouldn't surprise me to see some little freshman wearing it."

"Well, if they can take out other girls, we can go with other boys," said Irma in her soft voice.

"Hm . . . m . . . m! Easier said than done! Girls have to wait to be asked."

"Besides, we've cut ourselves off from several of

the best boys in the class. Look at Stan Moore and Joe Willard! They're certainly the leading juniors and not even in our Crowd. And we've lost Tony."

There was a sharp, rather significant silence.

"Tony is suspended again," Alice said.

"What happened?"

"I hate to say it, but I believe he came to school when he'd been drinking. He goes into the saloons sometimes with that fast gang he runs with."

"He's going around with a perfectly awful girl."

Betsy felt as though a hand had closed over her heart. She was silent through a regretful chorus of remarks that it was a shame, that Tony was an old peach and that something ought to be done about him. When the party ended she walked down the hill with the girls who were singing in parts

"You are my rose of Mexico. . . ."

Walking back alone through the April night, which held the sweetness of spring in spite of the cold, she seemed to hear Tony singing as he had sung so often beside the Ray piano. She remembered his indulgent, teasing fondness with the Crowd.

Tony had needed the Crowd. He had grown up too soon; he had been exposed to too many things too young, and it had made him a little bitter. On the other hand it had given him the experience, the sense of proportion which had enabled him to see the truth about fraternities. The others would have done well to have followed his lead in rejecting them.

But boys and girls who are old for their age need to be with people who are younger and sillier than they are. The Crowd, the normal happy high school Crowd, had been good for Tony. He had needed them, and they had let him down.

"I let him down," Betsy thought. "It was me especially, because Tony likes me. You might almost say he loves me, in a sort of way. I don't know how I'm going to do it, but I'm going to get Tony back. I'll have to manage to break up the fraternity and sorority first, though."

As it happened Betsy didn't need to take the initiative in that direction. In the Social Room next day Carney drew her aside.

"Miss Bangeter," she said, "has asked me to come to her office after school. I can't imagine what it's about. But I know it isn't anything pleasant."

"I'll go with you," Betsy offered, "wait outside the door and carry away your remains."

She waited, and Carney came out of Miss Bangeter's room looking flushed and embarrassed.

"It was about Okto Delta," she said. "She wishes we would break it up. She thinks Greek letter organizations are bad enough in college but in high school they're out of the question."

"What about the boys?" Betsy asked.

"They formed Omega Delta just to keep up with us. And she thinks it won't last long. It's the Okto Deltas she's worried about. I hope you won't mind, Betsy, but I promised her I'd urge you girls to end it."

"Heck!" said Betsy. "I'm willing. And I think everyone else is. It's been so much fun that I'd like to see it go before it's spoiled."

"So would I," said Carney.

"We'll just get together and agree to break it up."

"Sic transit Gloria," said Carney, which Betsy thought was most impressive. Carney went on earnestly, "I'd kind of like to square things with the school before I graduate. I think I'll give a party and invite the kids in our Crowd along with a lot of others—Stan, Hazel, Joe, and Phyllis Brandish. What do you say?"

"I think it's a good idea," said Betsy.

So Okto Delta, which had been born on a golden autumn hillside, disappeared with the last of the winter's frost. It melted away and was no more, and the pins were lost, or dropped into jewel cases and forgotten, or given away to boys who forgot to return them. Okto Delta went out with the school year.

The school year speeded up, as it always did in May. The members of the Domestic Science class entertained their mothers at a luncheon: cream of corn soup, croutons, croquettes, baked potato on the half shell, biscuits, salad, ice cream with toasted marshmallows, cakes and coffee.

The juniors were working furiously getting ready for the banquet. Betsy had told Hazel her idea about turning the school into a park.

"Why, that would be wonderful!" Hazel cried.

"Maybe you can think of something better," Betsy said, trying to be modest.

"No, I can't, nor of anything half so good."

Betsy's idea of a park was being carried out under Hazel's efficient direction.

The Inter-Society track meet was held and the cup went to the Philos. Since they had already secured the debating cup, much hung on the Essay Contest. Joe and Stan wrote their essays in mid-May. Betsy, herself, had no doubt as to the outcome. The Philomathians would win all three cups and it was her fault.

"I could have won the Essay Contest this year. Well, I'll win it next year or I'll know the reason why. There won't be any Okto Delta to keep me from getting the chance."

Folly was pretty well erased from their lives, but the consequences of folly were still with them.

21

The Consequences of Folly

"I DON'T KNOW WHY," said Betsy, "but I just didn't take all Gaston's talk about herbariums very seriously."

"Neither did I," said Tacy.

"Neither did I," said Tib. "But I don't see why we didn't. The very first day of school he gave us instructions about them, and he's mentioned them regularly ever since."

"We bought the paper covers and the glue and things ages ago."

"But then we forgot all about them."

"And now he wants them turned in tomorrow and he says they will count for one fourth of our year's marks! It's awful!" said Betsy, summarizing. "It's a perfectly awful situation!"

They were walking home from school in a mood of acute depression. A spell of warm rain had been followed by heat. The girls had changed that noon into thin, elbow-sleeved dresses. It was suddenly almost summer.

The rest of the Crowd had gone riding in Carney's auto, but Betsy, Tacy and Tib had not been able to go. They had come face to face at last with the matter of herbariums.

"'A herbarium,'" said Betsy, "'is a collection of dried and pressed specimens of plants, usually mounted or otherwise prepared for permanent preservation and systematically arranged in paper covers placed in boxes or cases.'"

"You know the definition all right," said Tib. "But you can't turn in a definition tomorrow."

"How many flowers did he say we had to have?"

"Fifty."

"We might as well tell him we haven't made them and all flunk the course," said practical Tib. "At least we'll be together when we repeat it next year."

"But I can't bear to flunk such an easy course. It's a disgrace!" groaned Tacy.

"Besides that," said Betsy. "I have to get some physics in sometime if I'm going to college."

Their footsteps echoed in a gloomy silence.

Then Betsy stopped. "See here!" she cried. "We're not going to give in. It's just four o'clock now and we have until nine tomorrow to make those herbariums. That's seventeen hours."

"Only nine," said Tib. "We're supposed to spend eight of them sleeping."

"*Supposed* to spend! *Supposed* to spend!" Betsy was scornful. "There's no law about going to bed the night you have to make a herbarium for botany. You both know as well as I do that the Big Hill is simply covered with flowers. We could find fifty different kinds between now and nine o'clock tomorrow."

"But, Betsy," said Tib. "We don't have to just pick them. We have to dry them and press them and paste them up and label them."

"All the harder," said Betsy triumphantly.

"All the harder! It's so hard it's impossible."

"No, it isn't. We'll have to stay at your house all night. We'll go up on the hill right now and pick until it gets dark, and then we'll go to your house and press the things we've found and paste them up.

We can label all night long."

Tacy's eyes began to shine. "Let's try. It would be fun."

"All right," said Tib. "I'm willing if you are. You can come, I think, but we can't let Papa and Mamma know we're awake all night."

They stopped in at the Ray house to telephone. Mrs. Muller didn't object to guests.

"Don't save supper for us," Tib said. "We want to get some flowers for our herbariums so we'll be out on the hill quite late. We'll fix ourselves something to eat when we come in. Don't worry if it's after dark."

Mrs. Ray said that Betsy might stay with Tib to "finish" her herbarium. They walked to Hill Street for Mrs. Kelly's permission, which they also secured. Filling their pockets with cookies and cheese—cheese, Betsy informed them, was very appropriate for such an expedition, being highly nourishing—they went up to the Big Hill.

It was the most enchanting moment of the spring. The heat had brought out little light green leaves on all the trees. Wild plum trees were in bloom, white and fragrant. They were full of bees and the grasses were full of flowers.

The girls picked industriously. They had all provided themselves with boxes and at first these seemed to fill with remarkable speed. They found clover and dandelions, and strawberry blossoms and buttercups, and wild geranium and lupine, and columbine and false Solomon's-seal.

"It's not going to be hard to find fifty different kinds at this rate," said Betsy. "Let's sit down and eat some of that nourishing cheese."

Tacy agreed but Tib warned, "We mustn't rest but a moment. It's getting late." The sun was, indeed, sinking toward the roof of Tacy's house.

They jumped up again presently. Like bird dogs on a scent they scurried in zigzag lines up the hill, picking as they went. Now they didn't seem to find many flowers they had not already found. There were purple violets.

"What about the dog-tooth kind?"

"There are plenty on top of the hill," Tacy said. They reached the top and started searching underneath the trees. They found the dog-tooth violets and spring beauties and wake-robins.

"Are the bloodroots all gone?"

"We might find just three. Here are some Dutchman's-breeches. One for each of us."

They found some ancient hepaticas, too.

Crossing the top of the hill, they dipped into the shadowy ravine. They found jacks-in-the-pulpit. They scrambled down to the stream where iris ought to be in bloom. It was. But twilight had caught up with them now. It was very dark in the ravine.

"How many have you got?" asked Tib.

"I've lost count," said Betsy.

"I have twenty-four, I think," said Tacy.

"I have thirty-two," said Tib. "And it's too dark to hunt any longer. We couldn't see anything now but a sunflower or something so big it would come up and hit us in the face."

"We'd better go home," said Betsy. "We'll get these pressed and pasted up and labeled. Then we'll set an alarm and be up and out with the sunrise. That's the best we can do."

"Maybe," suggested Tacy, "we could sneak in a few garden flowers? There are pansies around our house, and some bleeding hearts, and peonies. Lilacs, too."

"We'll certainly use them. If Gaston doesn't like it, it's just too bad," said Betsy.

Walking down the hill they finished the cookies and cheese. It was growing cool. Birds were calling to each other from tree to tree, and the west was full of gold-edged clouds.

They stopped at the Kellys' for Tacy's "dream robe," though she knew she'd have no need for it tonight. They proceeded to the Mullers', and to Tib's relief her father and mother were going out.

"Get yourselves plenty to eat now," Mrs. Muller

cautioned them. "Matilda left something for you."

"How does it happen you have to work so late. Eh?" Mr. Muller asked. "Couldn't you have collected these flowers earlier?"

"Not the spring flowers," said Tib. She tried to be vague about the whole thing. "We have to turn these herbariums in tomorrow, so we'll be pretty busy this evening."

"Well, get to bed by ten," said Mrs. Muller departing.

By ten! By ten their work was barely started. Flowers didn't dry, they discovered, simply by lying inside the dictionary for half an hour.

"We'll have to dry them in the oven," Tib decided They went down to the kitchen and lit the oven and put their flowers in.

Tib's brothers, Frederick and Hobbie, took a friendly interest. Fred lighted a lantern and went out to the vacant lot behind the house. He brought back quite a handful of weeds. Encouraged by their praise, he took the lantern and went out again—with Hobbie this time—and brought back another handful.

"This work has to be systematized," said Betsy. "We can't all sit here waiting for the flowers to bake. I'll take charge of that, and Tib can start pasting up the ones that are dried, and Tacy can start looking them up in the botany books."

"*Liebchen*," said Tib. "We can't trust you to sit by

the fire while the flowers bake. You'd get to thinking about something else and let them all burn."

"I'll watch them," Freddie offered.

"That would be good," said Tib. "Freddie is very reliable."

So Fred and Hobbie sat by the oven watching the flowers bake and bringing them upstairs when they reached the proper state of dryness. Tacy and Tib, more deft with their fingers than Betsy, pasted rapidly while Betsy tried to identify the various specimens by consulting the botany books.

Everything was going beautifully when the Mullers' returning carriage was heard outside. The oven was hastily extinguished along with the kitchen light, and the flowers were hustled upstairs. Fred and Hobbie dashed to their room and into bed with their clothes on. The girls turned out their light, too, and when Mr. and Mrs. Muller came upstairs Tib called, "Good night. You don't need to bother to wake us. I've taken the alarm clock."

"It seems to me you could have done some of this work earlier in the season," Mr. Muller grumbled, but the girls pretended not to hear him. When the house was dark and quiet, they cautiously lighted the gas.

Finding the flowers had been hard and drying them even harder, but labeling them proved to be hardest of all. It was easy enough to track down violets and

Dutchman's-breeches, columbine and wild geranium. But some of the weeds Fred and Hobbie had brought in from the vacant lot defied classification. Midnight passed, and one o'clock and two o'clock. They were still working.

"I'm going to get some sleep," said Tib, "and I advise you to do the same. I've set the alarm for five."

So they all lay down on Tib's bed, pulling a comforter over their tired bodies.

It seemed to Betsy that she had hardly closed her eyes before the alarm clock was shrilling. Tib shut it off quickly and they tiptoed into the bathroom to splash their faces before combing their hair. There was no time for puffs today.

"I'd like a cup of coffee," Betsy said, but there wasn't time even for that. They paused in the kitchen to light the oven; they would have to dry whatever flowers they found before Matilda came down to get breakfast. Putting on their jackets, they stole out of doors.

Color was streaking the sky and birds were competing in mad chorus, but the girls were too sleepy to observe the beauty of the dawn. They reached the vacant lot and Tib stooped to begin picking, but then she uttered a disgusted exclamation.

"*Drei Dummkopfen!* That's what we are."

"What's the matter?"

"Flowers don't open until the sun comes up!"

Betsy and Tacy dropped to their knees and they saw that the humble herbage was indeed a soggy indistinguishable mass. There might or might not be blossoms later on these wet and tightly coiled grasses.

"Fine botany students we are!" cried Tacy and went off into laughter which made the robins, thrashers, meadow larks and warblers redouble their efforts at vocal supremacy.

"We might as well have had our coffee," burbled Betsy. "We have to sit here until the sun comes up."

"No," said Tib. "We'll grab handfuls just like Fred and Hobbie did last night. We can see later whether any flowers appear."

"It will add to the suspense," said Tacy, wiping laughter from her eyes, and they all began to pick. They picked until Tib said, "We simply must have fifty kinds now."

They tiptoed into the kitchen and put their scurvy specimens into the oven. Tib made coffee while they baked. Taking weeds and coffee up to Tib's room, they started pasting and labeling again.

"We can't possibly identify all these," said Tib.

"Some of them," said Tacy, "will have to remain forever anonymous."

"I know," said Betsy. "We'll make a point of the fact that we can't identify them. 'Mr. Gaston,' we will say, 'What are these rare and interesting specimens?

We can't find them in any of our learned tomes.'"

They were all feeling silly but as the sun climbed higher and the need to complete their work grew urgent they fell silent and even grim.

Mrs. Muller knocked at the door. "Are you awake?"

"Oh, yes. We've been down and had our breakfast. Tell Matilda not to be surprised if the oven is hot."

At eight o'clock they stumbled out of the house, rumpled, pale, with lines beneath their eyes and herbariums under their arms.

"I think," said Tib, as they walked down Hill Street, "that this was an idiotic thing to do."

Betsy and Tacy grunted.

"Why, I realized last night that I would have enjoyed making a herbarium. I like to do that sort of thing. I could have made a good one."

"So could I," admitted Tacy.

"Well, I couldn't," said Betsy. "But I should have been interested, at least. I'm crazy enough about flowers."

"As a matter of fact," said Tib, "we've had a pretty foolish year. You and I especially, Betsy. It's been fun, and I guess it's been worth it but I wouldn't want another year this foolish."

"Neither would I," said Tacy.

"Me either," said Betsy.

"We're getting a little old for this sort of thing," said Tib, looking severe.

22

The Junior-Senior Banquet

THE JUNIOR-SENIOR BANQUET was drawing near now and Betsy, Tacy and Tib—herbariums and exams disposed of—were working hard on the decorating committee.

It usually met at the Ray house.

"You can just as well meet here. It's so convenient

to school," Betsy had said, and now, as a matter of course, Hazel Smith came in with Tacy and Tib almost every day.

Tib was only an ex-officio member of the committee, but her small artistic fingers made her invaluable.

"My right-hand woman!" Hazel declared.

The four went downtown to buy favors for the fish pond, tissue paper, cardboard for signs. They returned to the Rays' to make fudge or poach eggs, according to their moods and appetites.

Cab and Dennie declared themselves ex-officio members also. Cab covered himself with glory with a NO FLIRTING ALLOWED sign for Lovers' Lane. Margaret wrapped packages happily for the fish pond. One night Hazel, Tacy and Tib stayed all night, spreading from Betsy's into Julia's room, frantically talking Junior-Senior Banquet. It was almost, but not quite, like making herbariums.

Even in the midst of this excitement, Betsy could not forget about Tony. There was a sore place in her heart because of him. He wasn't in school. He had not come to the Rays' for several weeks, and the night before the banquet she telephoned him.

"Can't you come to lunch Sunday night?"

"Sorry. I've got a date."

"What do you mean, having a date on Sunday night? Papa's feelings are hurt."

"I'll bet," Tony replied. There was a brief silence. Then he said, "Maybe your father wouldn't even want me to come? Has he heard about the mess I'm in?"

"My father," Betsy replied, "says you're the only boy who comes to the house who really appreciates his sandwiches. He's clamoring for you, Tony."

"Really?" Tony sounded pleased.

"You show up!" Betsy said. "That's an order. And by the way"—she tried hard to be casual—"don't you want me to save a dance for you at the banquet?"

"I'm not going," Tony said.

"Tony Markham! Not coming to your own Junior-Senior Banquet? You must be crazy."

"You know I've been suspended."

"Suspended isn't expelled. You'll probably be suspended more than once before you graduate. How many dances shall I save?"

"Do you dance with a barb?"

"Evidently," said Betsy, "you haven't been keeping up with school affairs. There aren't any Greek letter organizations at Deep Valley High any more. They're ended. They're *kaput*."

There was another silence, longer this time.

"Is that straight?" Tony asked.

"Of course it is. We all got tired of the things, and besides Miss Bangeter called us down. You aren't the only one who gets called down, you know. We were fools ever to start them, Tony. They lost us all the good committee appointments this spring. They lost me the chance to try out for the Essay Contest. You were the only one in the Crowd with any sense, when you turned thumbs down."

Tony replied quickly this time. His big deep laugh rolled out over the 'phone.

"Sure you can save me some dances," he said. "Two of them. Both waltzes, please. Say, Betsy! You haven't forgotten how to waltz?"

"You'll see," Betsy replied.

Junior-Senior Banquet day dawned hot. It was, by some freak of Minnesota weather, ninety in the shade, but the juniors were too conscious of their responsibilities even to know that it was hot. Wearing their oldest clothes, sleeves rolled up for action, they moved into the high school in a body.

Down in the Domestic Science room aprons were being donned, ovens were being lighted, egg beaters were whirling.

Stan, in overalls, went about chanting his speech, the "Farewell to the Seniors" he had to deliver that night.

Lloyd had brought his auto, and he and Tib and Hazel drove to the woods for boughs of blooming trees. Betsy and Tacy, putting up signs, pounded until their fingers were blue. They dragged settees, pushed tables, ran upstairs and down.

Rain began, and the palms which were to make Lovers' Lane had not arrived. Hazel stared at Betsy and Tacy in misery, and Dave, who was making the fish pond—pants rolled up and hair on end—offered to go out and chop down some trees. But the palms came after all.

And so at last did six o'clock. Tantalizing odors were rising from the Domestic Science room. It was time to go home and dress.

The decorating committee paused for a final proud look. The park was a bower of flowery green. A swing rocked in one shady corner. Lovers' Lane led cool and inviting up the stairs.

Betsy put her arm around Hazel. "It looks beautiful," she said.

"It was a wonderful idea of yours, Betsy."

"You were the big executive who carried it out."

Stan joined them and Betsy lifted a dirty but radiant face.

"It's going to make history, Stan. The banquet given by the class of 1910 will never be forgotten."

"You've worked hard," said Stan. "All your Crowd has."

Betsy knew that this was an apology.

"Save a dance for me," he said.

"I will," she promised.

At home she bathed and dressed hurriedly. Her mother asked whether Dave had, by any chance, signified his intention of calling for her and Betsy said he hadn't.

"I think he will though," she added.

Strangely enough, she didn't care very much. It would not seem tragic if she went to the banquet alone or with a bunch of girls. She was thinking about the park. How Carney and the other seniors would rave about it!

"We did a grand job!" she exclaimed to her family.

Dave appeared at eight o'clock, immaculate, every hair in place.

"You look a little different than you did an hour ago," said Betsy, smiling.

Appraising Betsy in the old rose dress he actually answered.

"So do you," he said.

The tables in the Domestic Science room gleamed with borrowed linen and silver. Irma, Alice and Winona, in ruffled aprons, served. The program committee, headed by Joe Willard, had provided little booklets which he had had printed at the *Deep Valley Sun*. They included the menu, the list of speeches, and the dance program.

Thanks to Joe, perhaps, the menu had a highly intellectual flavor.

*"Now good digestion wait on appetite and
health on both."*—SHAKESPEARE
Fruit Cocktail

"Can one desire too much of a good thing?"—CERVANTES
Roast Lamb and Mashed Potatoes
Mint Jelly
Peas in Timbale Cases
Olives
Rolls
Nuts

"My appetite comes to me while eating."—MONTAIGNE
Tomato and Asparagus Salad
Cheese and Crackers

"Then farewell heat and welcome frost."—SHAKESPEARE
Ice Cream
Cakes
Coffee
Candy

After the dinner there were toasts. Miss Bangeter
spoke on "The Event," and told of past Junior-Senior
Banquets. Stan, transformed as Dave was and completely poised, toasted the seniors. He did better, the
juniors thought, than the senior girl who returned
the toast.

The company repaired to the park to swing and fish in the pond and flirt along Lovers' Lane. Programs for the dance were filled out—Betsy's was completed in no time—and Mamie Dodd began to play the piano in the upper hall, which had been kept clear for dancing.

Betsy came out of the girls' cloak room to which she had repaired to freshen her hair and put powder on her face. She was very happy. She knew she would be tired tomorrow, but the park had been worth it. It had been a glorious success.

Besides, Tony had come and claimed his two waltzes. He had not come for the dinner and she had been worried, but he had arrived for the dancing, looking exceptionally well pressed and well groomed. Miss Bangeter had crossed the room to speak to him.

Waiting for Dave, who had taken the first dance, Betsy saw Joe Willard break away from a group across the room and come toward her. He had never asked her for a dance. In fact, she didn't think he had ever danced with any girl in school except Phyllis. He and Phyllis had always dropped into high school parties too late to fill out programs. As a result they had always danced just with each other and had usually left early. Tonight they had been present when the programs were filled out. There was no reason, Betsy thought, why he should not have asked her for a dance. But he hadn't.

However, he was coming toward her purposefully now.

He looked happy. All the juniors were happy to-night. His pompadour looked very high and light above his dark blue suit.

"May I have a dance, Miss Ray?"

"Why did you have to be so slow? My program is all full," said Betsy and waited fearfully remembering how sensitive Joe had always been. But evidently he had lost that chip he used to carry on his shoulder. Going with Phyllis had made him . . . suave, she thought.

"That was dumb of Willard!" he answered cheer-fully.

This was reassuring but nevertheless Betsy was determined not to let him go.

In her freshman year he had asked to walk home with her from a party and she had had to turn him down. After a long time he had asked to walk home with her from the library one evening. Again she had had to turn him down.

"This would be three times and out," she thought. "I have to break this jinx."

She smiled. "I'm going to give you a dance," she said. "Some of these people who took two can just give one up."

"Good!" said Joe. "That's the spirit I like to see.

Who shall we steal from?" He took her program and studied it. "Markham has the best disposition."

"But I like him the best!" protested Betsy. "Tony is a great favorite of mine."

"Who shall it be then?"

"Lloyd. He only took two because Tib was mad at him, and I think she's relenting. When he comes to get me we'll just say there's been a mix-up."

"Mix-up Willard," said Joe, writing down his name. The stolen dance was the eleventh one, the next to the last. His program, except for the eleventh dance, bore only a sprawling perpendicular "Phyllis."

Carney had just come out of the girls' cloak room.

"Did I hear you scratch a dance for Joe Willard?" she asked. "Do you remember telling me that he didn't mean anything to you but the Essay Contest?"

Betsy flushed and smiled.

"What's up?" asked Winona, joining them.

"Joe Willard just asked Betsy for a dance."

"Really? Phyllis won't like this!" Winona took a look at Betsy's program. "Bet a nickel she'll make him go home before we reach number eleven."

The evening sped along from waltz to two-step, from schottische to barn dance.

"I must admit you can still waltz. It's all because I took you in hand when you were young," said Tony.

Betsy had glanced at his program. He was dancing with Tacy, Irma, Carney. She felt with thankfulness that she had taken the first step toward rescuing Tony, although he was not yet out of danger.

At the end of the second waltz she said, "See you for Sunday night lunch?"

"I hope your father has plenty of onions in the house," Tony replied.

His black eyes were teasing, but she knew that he would come.

"I hear," Hazel remarked to Betsy, "that Joe Willard has asked you for a dance."

"What's this about Joe Willard asking you to dance?" Tacy inquired.

"Has Joe Willard really asked you for a dance?" questioned Tib.

"Heavens!" said Betsy. "News spreads fast around this high school."

"I even heard that you scratched a dance to give him one," said Tib.

"Maybe the *Deep Valley Sun* would like a story about it," Betsy replied.

She realized presently that the great news must have reached Phyllis. Phyllis and Joe were standing at the cloak room door engaged in what was plainly an altercation. Betsy couldn't hear what they were saying but from their expressions, the growing tenseness of the conversation, she felt she could interpret it.

Phyllis had said that she wanted to go home; Joe had objected.

"Why, we always go home early," Betsy could imagine Phyllis saying.

Joe would be casual. "Oh, let's wait a little while!"

"I'd like to go now if you don't mind."

"Well, look, Phyllis. I have a date. And she scratched another fellow's dance to give me one."

"Really? Well, you may do as you like. *I'm* going home."

Betsy didn't hear this conversation but she must have imagined it with some degree of exactness, for Phyllis went into the cloak room and came out with her pale green opera cape, and Joe held it for her and they went down the stairs.

In five minutes the news had spread around the hall. Joe Willard had asked Betsy Ray for a dance. She had scratched off a name to give him one and then Phyllis wouldn't let him stay for it.

"I'm afraid Phyllis is boss," Carney whispered regretfully.

"I think he'll come back," Betsy said.

The tenth dance ended and there followed the brief intermission during which boys took leave of their old partners and sought new ones. Betsy waited for Joe. He did not come.

Mamie Dodd started to play the piano. It was a new song Betsy liked.

> *"The girl I'll call my sweetheart,*
> *Must look like you. . . ."*

Couples moved out to the floor, circled. Still Joe didn't come.

Betsy stood alone. She would stand there only a moment. She knew the proper thing to do if you were stranded without a partner, although she had seldom found herself in that undesirable predicament. She started to move toward the cloak room but first her eyes circled the hall and she saw Joe almost running up the stairs.

His mouth smiled but his eyes were stormy and rebellious. He looked as though he had come from a battle. Betsy knew that he had taken Phyllis to her automobile but had refused to go home before the eleventh dance.

Betsy smiled. Joe put his arm around her and they moved out onto the dance floor. He danced well, not smoothly like Dave, nor with Tony's rhythmic skill but with zest and in perfect time. He whirled her as she had never been whirled before.

She was glad to be whirled. It was a triumph to be dancing with Joe Willard. Yet it wasn't just triumph which filled her.

"Does it mean anything?" she wondered. "For next year, of course."

Joe would not, she felt sure, desert Phyllis now, even though they had had a disagreement. He was a fundamentally loyal person. He had been unwilling to humiliate Betsy by leaving her without a partner, and he would certainly not humiliate Phyllis, with whom he had had such a good time all year, by deserting her at the beginning of a gay Commencement week—when she was a senior, too. He would see her through.

But maybe, just the same, he didn't care about her any more. Maybe he never had.

"I wonder, what about next year," thought Betsy, whirling in Joe Willard's arms.

23

Tar

"PERHAPS IT WASN'T such a good idea to rouse the Philos' fighting spirit by putting up that pennant last fall," Carney said.

A group of Zet girls sat together on the alcove bookcase in the high school auditorium. This was gay with Zetamathian blue and Philomathian orange. It was the evening assembly at which the Essay Cup would be awarded.

Always a great occasion, opening Commencement week, this year it held unusual importance. The Philomathians had already won in debating and athletics. If they won the Essay Cup tonight they would have the almost unprecedented honor of holding all three cups.

Betsy found it exciting to be sitting with the others. In her freshman and sophomore years she had been a contestant, and so had sat in regal aloofness on the platform. Down in the teeming, turbulent, rumor-filled auditorium, suspense enveloped her and hemmed her in. It was terrible to think that the Philos might win tonight, but Betsy agreed with Carney that there was danger.

"Joe Willard," she declared, "will win over Stan."

She was a good prophet. The freshman points went to the Philos. The sophomore points went to the Philos. Then, before a screaming, cheering crowd, Joe Willard for the third year in succession was announced to have won his class points. He stood up to take the applause, his yellow hair shining, his face shining, too, with pleasure.

No matter where the senior points went, the Philos had won now, and they almost went mad with joy.

"Philo, Philo, Philo
Philomathian. . . . Wow!"

"Poor old Zet. Poor old Zet!"

And, of course;

"What's the matter with Willard?
He's all right."

Betsy felt mixed emotions. As a Zetamathian she was crushed. This year, she felt sure, she could have been the deciding factor in winning the Essay Contest. The third orange bow, which Miss Bangeter was tying now, reproached and mocked her. On the other hand, liking Joe as she did, she couldn't help rejoicing in his moment of splendid triumph.

The next morning report cards were given out. Tacy and Tib called for Betsy. They met Cab and Dennie on High Street, and just as she had done the previous fall, Tacy cried out suddenly, "What's that crowd doing in front of the high school? Is it on fire?"

"Gosh!" said Cab. "It would be wasteful to have it burn down now when examinations are over."

Something remarkable was going on, for the crowd pushed from the school lawn out into the street. Everyone was looking up at the roof, and Cab and Dennie began to run.

"Were you up on that roof again last night?" Tib cried.

"Heck, no! and neither was Dave!"

But it developed shortly that not Cab nor Dennie nor Dave could possibly have been suspected of this skulduggery. Giant letters were painted on the high school roof. But the paint was orange. The letters spelled out PHILOMATHIAN.

"How could anyone have painted on that steep roof?"

"They must have had a ladder."

"See that strip of black paint underneath."

But it wasn't black paint, they discovered when they reached the school house.

"It's tar. It was put on so no Zetamathian boy could reach the letters and paint them out. Dave Hunt shinnied up to the cupola, all the way to the roof, but then he discovered the tar. He almost got stuck in it."

"He must be mad," Betsy cried.

"Not so mad as Miss Bangeter."

Miss Bangeter, the students discovered when a furiously clanging gong had brought them into the high school, was really angry. She did not even announce an opening song. Tall and terrible, her black eyes flashing beneath the high twist of black hair, she came to the front of the platform.

"Last fall a Zetamathian pennant was put up on the roof," she said. "The perpetrator was reprimanded and it was explained to the whole school that it was dangerous to attempt to climb the high school roof. But last night, as you have all seen, this rule was disobeyed. Will all the Philomathian boys in the school please rise?"

There was a clatter as more than a hundred boys rose to their feet.

"Will you form a line and march past me?"

They formed a line and marched. Carney did not play a tune. The procession wasn't exhilarating and gay. It was awkward, anxious, slow; and it soon became slower.

"It isn't likely," Miss Bangeter said, when the line reached the platform, "that the boys who spread that tar on the roof could have done it without getting some on their own feet. Will each boy stop as he passes my desk and show me the bottom of his shoes?"

The long line filed past her. As each boy passed he stopped and lifted his feet. Now and then Miss Bangeter asked one to step out of line. The others returned to their seats. At the end there were three boys standing beside her. They were Squirrelly, Tony, and Joe.

Squirrelly looked innocent as he always did. Tony's

eyes were laughing. Joe Willard's lips were compressed.

"I take it," said Miss Bangeter, "that you three boys painted the letters on the roof?"

"I did," said Squirrelly.

"I did," said Tony, in his deep voice.

"I didn't," said Joe, and after a wave of surprise which rolled over the assembly room had subsided he said with a broad grin, "I spread the tar."

Miss Bangeter's lips twitched.

"You three may come to my office after school," she said.

Punishment, every one knew, would be severe and it was. The three boys were suspended, but that was a formality, since school was already over. They were obliged, however, to pay for having the letters and the tar removed and that proved to be expensive. Workmen swarmed up tall ladders with buckets and brooms but it was a long time before the orange Philomathian and the black band of tar were erased from the Deep Valley High School roof. In fact, the tar never quite came off.

Report cards were an anti-climax, although Betsy was pleased to find that most of her grades had improved. Miss Fowler raised her to 95; Miss Clarke, grieving about the Essay Contest, perhaps, gave her 93; Miss Erickson, forgiving the "old pill" incident, conceded her 90.

Mr. Gaston awarded a grim 75 to Betsy, to Tacy and to Tib.

"Never, never in my whole life," said Mr. Gaston, (he was twenty-four), "never in my whole career as a teacher," (he had taught for three years), "have I seen such herbariums! Not a fall flower included!"

But he felt a little guilty, perhaps because he could not identify all the specimens they had presented. At any rate, for whatever reason, he passed them.

The chorus was practising in the Opera House for Commencement.

"I heard the trailing garments of the night,
    Sweep through her marble halls!
    I saw her sable skirts all fringed with light. . . ."

Betsy loved that song, and it wove itself through the events of the torrid June week when Julia, back from the U, was getting ready to sail away to Europe and Carney was getting ready to graduate. Carney's hard work had not been for nothing. She had been accepted for Vassar.

"We . . . are . . . the class of oh-nine," sang Carney, Al, Squirrelly and the rest of the seniors on Class Day to the now familiar tune of "Old, Old is Honeymoon Trail." Then Commencement was upon them.

The Opera House was crowded with proud relatives

and friends, and the graduates sat on the platform with the chorus behind them.

"I heard the trailing garments of the night," sang Betsy and Tacy. There were speeches; Carney made one of them. And the seniors crossed the stage one by one, received their diplomas while loyal hands applauded.

Phyllis in a white lace dress carried a big bouquet of roses. It came from Joe, Betsy felt sure, but she did not see Joe in the audience. Phil came right behind his sister looking sheepishly pleased, not sulky at all.

Carney came, her dimple showing, and she, too, carried roses.

"Do you know who sent Carney her bouquet?"

"Al Larson, I suppose."

"No. It was Larry Humphreys. He's been out in California three years now, but he hasn't forgotten her."

Carney received a large number of presents but none of them, she assured Betsy, was more cherished than the jabot which Betsy finished and delivered, wrapped in tissue paper and ribbon, along with a silver spoon.

"It's very nice," said Carney smoothing the tortured looking object. "I'm going to take it to Vassar with me."

"Will you wear it?"

"I promised to. Didn't I? But just once! Then I'll hang it up as a souvenir."

After the graduating exercises Mr. and Mrs. Sibley gave a party for Carney. It was the one Carney had suggested the day she and Betsy agreed to break up Okto Delta. The Crowd was invited along with many other friends—Hazel and Stan and the Brandishes and Joe.

It was a beautiful party. There was punch in a big crystal bowl. There were little frosted cakes. Young and old moved happily through the front and back parlor and the library of the Sibleys' spacious house. Betsy kept looking for Joe Willard. But he wasn't there.

"He's left for the summer," Carney explained when Betsy asked her at last. "He's going to the harvest fields again."

Betsy wished she had seen him before he left.

"Cab isn't here either," Irma remarked.

"No," answered Carney, looking serious. "He telephoned early this evening. His father has gone to the hospital."

24
Growing Up

CAB'S FATHER DIED. He had been ill for some time, and Mrs. Ray had been sending cakes, pies and hot casserole dishes over to the Edwards family, who lived less than a block away. First he was ill at home and then he was removed to the hospital. One day in mid-June Dennie came into the Ray house to say,

"Mr. Edwards died last night. I was down at the hospital with Cab."

Dennie looked as though he hadn't slept. His curly hair was more than ordinarily rumpled and his eyes were swelled. He didn't have the jaunty carefree look which usually characterized both him and Cab.

The Rays grew suddenly sober, as people in a happy home do when death strikes in another happy home. Betsy didn't know Cab's father very well. She knew he was stern but also just and kind, and that Cab's mother was a gentle, somewhat helpless woman, and that there were several younger children.

The Crowd sent flowers and many of them went to the funeral. Betsy went with her father and mother. The Edwards' house seemed odd and unfamiliar, with folding chairs set out in the parlor, the air heavy with the scent of flowers. Betsy caught a glimpse of Cab in a dark, well-pressed suit, looking pale but composed and manly. He kept close hold of the arm of his mother, whose face was hidden under a thick black veil. The little sisters sat with some of the older relatives. Betsy saw Cab turn and look at them once or twice, especially when the littlest sister cried.

Two days later, when Betsy was baking a Domestic Science plum cake, he came in at the kitchen door. He seemed almost like his usual self and remarked, sniffing, that something smelled good.

"And I produced it!" Betsy said. "Anna is busy washing and ironing for Julia. She leaves the last of the week, you know."

"How soon will it be done?" asked Cab.

"In time to give you a piece."

She couldn't bring herself to mention his father but when they went into the parlor her own father, coming in for dinner, referred to his loss and Cab seemed glad to talk.

"My mother's been wonderful," he said.

"I just stopped in at your house," Mr. Ray replied. "She said the same thing about you."

Cab flushed. "There's been a lot to attend to," he said. "Not just the funeral. My uncle and aunt helped us to make arrangements for that. But Dad's store. . . . Somebody has to pitch in and take his place, and it looks as though it would be me."

"You mean this summer?" Betsy asked.

"Not just this summer." He addressed Mr. Ray. "You know old Mr. Loring has been Dad's clerk for years. He can take charge, but the business wouldn't justify hiring another clerk. I've worked there vacations. I'd fit in pretty well and at the same time I'd learn the business so that I could take over from Mr. Loring some day."

"You won't . . . go back to school?" Betsy could hardly take it in.

"Nope. Will you buy your furniture from me, Betsy?"

"But, Cab, you were going to be an engineer!"

"Mamma can't run the business. She has to take care of the kids."

"But . . . could you . . . can you. . . ."

"Heck!" said Cab. "I'm seventeen."

After dinner Betsy went up to her bedroom. She had cried at Cab's father's funeral. She didn't feel like crying now, but she had a heavy sick feeling.

"Cab isn't going to graduate. He wanted to, just as much as I do. He had all kinds of class spirit. But he's not even going back.

"He's taking over his father's store. And he's no older than I am. I wonder if I could do that if my father died—stop school, pitch in and help my mother."

She looked at herself closely in the mirror.

"I'm seventeen, but I've certainly not been acting it. How silly and kiddish we've all been this year! Well, it's all for over for Cab. He's grown up."

She sat down, knotting her hands tightly together, trying to think.

Cab was one of her best friends. Yesterday he had been as sheltered and carefree as she was. Now he had joined the ranks of those who, like Joe and Mamie Dodd, had no fathers to look after them.

"Just one thing happened. Something that could happen to anyone in a minute. His father dying has made all the difference."

It seemed strange and a little wonderful that Cab had been able to grow up so suddenly, that he had been able to produce when he needed it the strength to take care of his mother and little sisters.

"I don't suppose he knew he had it in him. I hope I have it in me. I hope I could pull out strength and courage like that if I found I needed to."

She got up and began to walk around again.

"Oh, I'm sorry, sorry that Cab is leaving school!"

"Betsy," called her mother. "Don't forget you have a music lesson." As Betsy came down the stairs Mrs. Ray said anxiously, "You look pale. Are you sure you feel able to go? I'll call Miss Cobb."

"Listen to that!" Betsy thought to herself. "My mother and father are always looking after me. I've got to start standing on my own two feet. I've got to start growing up, too."

"No, thanks," she said cheerfully. "I feel fine. I haven't practised a bit this week but I don't think Miss Cobb will expect it. She knows we're in a dither getting Julia off."

"She's busy with the same sort of thing, only less happy," Mrs. Ray said. "She's getting Leonard ready to go to Colorado. He hasn't been getting any better . . . he's been getting worse. So she's sending him out to the mountains."

"Will he get well, do you think, Mamma?"

"I hope so," Mrs. Ray said doubtfully. "But I'm glad young Bobby is so husky."

After her lesson Betsy went into the little back parlor to say good-by to Leonard. He looked even thinner than usual and his cheeks were like crimson tissue paper. But he laughed and joked, saying good-by to Betsy.

"Don't learn too much piano while I'm gone," he said. "I want you to be coming for lessons when I get home again."

"I'm practically a Paderewski this minute," Betsy answered. "I can play the 'Soul Kiss' music. But I intend to keep on studying just because I like your Auntie."

"I'm not surprised," said Leonard. "I like her myself."

He smiled at Miss Cobb, whose answering smile was as calm and cheerful as though he were going to St. John to play football instead of to the Colorado mountains to die.

"I hope he'll prove it by writing some letters," she said. "And not just the 'having-a-fine-time-hope-you-are-too' kind of letters. That's the sort he usually writes."

Betsy tried to imitate Miss Cobb's serene matter-of-factness.

"Will you write to me, too? If you do, and if what your aunt says is true, you'll get the best of the bargain. I write simply gigantic letters to Julia and to Herbert Humphreys out in California."

Leonard's face brightened. "I could use some long epistles like that while I'm in Colorado."

"See that you answer them," Betsy replied.

Leonard's brother Bobby passed her on the steps. He was rushing into the house, rosy and disheveled. Betsy knew why her mother was glad that Bobby was so husky. Miss Cobb would have one out of the four children she had raised.

"That's one promise I'm going to keep," Betsy muttered in an undertone, walking away. "I'm going to write to Leonard every week as long as he lives."

She walked up the hill toward her own home slowly, for the weather was still warm. The air smelled of roses in bloom in every dooryard. There were snow balls in bloom, too, white and luscious, and orioles were singing and whistling in the maples. Betsy kept thinking about Leonard and Cab.

When she reached home she found a postal card lying on the music room table. It lay face up and she saw the picture of the Main Street of a small north Texas town.

She turned it over and found that it was addressed to herself. It came from Joe Willard. He had written, "Did anyone ever tell you that you're a good dancer? Joe."

She stood for some time with the card in her hand before she went upstairs.

Her mother and Julia were busy with the trunk in Julia's room. They called "Hello" and she responded but she didn't join them. She went to her own room.

She put the card first in the handkerchief box where she always put notes from boys she was in love with, but after a few minutes she took it out. It didn't seem to belong there.

She stuck it into the mirror where she sometimes put dance programs and invitations and other gay things. She left it there a while but it didn't seem right there either.

She wandered over to Uncle Keith's trunk, her beloved desk. Above it hung a picture of a long-legged white bird which Herbert had sent her. She kept it above the trunk because it reminded her of Babcock's Bay out at Murmuring Lake.

Still holding the postal card from Joe, she stared at the bird reflectively.

All those resolutions she had made on Babcock's Bay! How they had been smashed to smithereens! She wondered whether life consisted of making resolutions and breaking them, of climbing up and slipping down.

"I believe that's it," she thought. "And the bright side of it is that you never slip down to quite the point you started climbing from. You always gain a little. This year I've gained my music lessons, and all the things Miss Fowler taught me about writing, and a postal card from Joe." That seemed funny to her and she laughed, but she grew serious again.

She thought about those lists she had made in her programs for self-improvement. She hadn't followed them out by any means, but they had revealed her ideals.

At first they had been mostly about brushing hair and teeth. Then she had reached out for charm: green bows, foreign phrases, perfumes, a bath every day. Last summer's resolves to be thoughtful at home and to excel at school, had shown a sort of groping after maturity.

"And this year," she thought. "I haven't even started a list. I've just realized definitely that there were things I wanted to do. . . ."

She was going to write to Leonard, to reach out for people like Hazel Smith, to get Tony away from that wild gang and keep him safe in the Crowd.

"Gosh!" she thought. "I must be growing up."

It came to her that there was more to growing up than drinking coffee at Heinz's.

The whole Crowd, she decided, was growing up. Carney had begun when she worked so hard on those entrance exams for Vassar. Tony had begun when he took his stand against fraternities, and even when he had that fling at wildness which Betsy hoped to end. Tacy had begun in her absorption in music and Tib, when she had seen so clearly how silly they had been about herbariums.

Cab, of course, had grown up more than any of them.

But all of them were growing up, Betsy thought intensely. They would never be quite so silly again. The foolish crazy things they had done this year they would do less and less frequently until they didn't do them at all.

"We're growing up," Betsy said aloud. She wasn't even sure she liked it. But it happened, and then it was irrevocable. There was nothing you could do about it except to try to see that you grew up into the kind of human being you wanted to be.

"I'd like to be a fine one," Betsy thought quickly and urgently.

Anna came up to Julia's bedroom with an armful of freshly pressed clothes for the trunk. Betsy could hear Julia's voice and Margaret's and her mother's. A second trunk stood open in Mrs. Ray's room, for the Ray family was going to the lake as soon as Julia sailed away. Betsy could almost smell the water lilies on Babcock's Bay. She opened the trunk and got out her novel.

"I'm going to finish this, although it's terrible. And I'm going to start another, better one; or maybe I'll do a short story first and send it to the *Delineator*. It's time I started selling my stories. Here! Here! Here!" she thought, laughing. "I'm making a list."

But perhaps people who liked to write always made lists! Just for the fun of it.

She heard the front door downstairs open and Tacy and Tib called, "Yoo hoo!"

"Yoo hoo! Come on up," called Betsy.

She put Joe Willard's postal card into Uncle Keith's trunk.

Maud Hart Lovelace and Her World

(Adapted from *The Betsy-Tacy Companion: A Biography of Maud Hart Lovelace* by Sharla Scannell Whalen)

Maud Palmer Hart circa 1906
Collection of Sharla Scannell Whalen

MAUD HART LOVELACE was born on April 25, 1892, in Mankato, Minnesota. Shortly after Maud's high school graduation in 1910, the Hart family left Mankato and settled in Minneapolis, where Maud attended the University of Minnesota. In 1917 she married Delos W. Lovelace, a newspaper reporter who later became a popular writer of short stories. The Lovelaces' daughter, Merian, was born in 1931.

Maud would tell her daughter bedtime stories about her childhood in Minnesota, and it was these stories that gave her the idea of writing the Betsy-Tacy books. She did not intend to write an entire series when *Betsy-Tacy*, the first book, was published in 1940, but readers asked for more stories. So Maud took Betsy through high school and beyond college to the "great world" and marriage.

The final book in the series, *Betsy's Wedding*, was published in 1955.

The Betsy-Tacy books are based very closely upon Maud's own life. "I could make it all up, but in these Betsy-Tacy stories, I love to work from real incidents," Maud wrote. This is especially true of the four high school books. We know a lot about her life during this period because Maud kept diaries (one for each high school year, just like Betsy) as well as a scrapbook during high school. As she wrote to a cousin in 1964: "In writing the high school books my diaries were extremely helpful. The family life, customs, jokes, traditions are all true and the general pattern of the years is also accurate."

Almost every character in the high school books, even the most minor, can be matched to an actual person living in Mankato in the early years of the twentieth century. (See page 301 for a list of characters and their real-life counterparts.) But there are exceptions. As Maud wrote: "A small and amusing complication is that while some of the characters are absolutely based on one person—for example Tacy, Tib, Cab, Carney—others were merely suggested by some person and some characters are combinations of two real persons." For example, the character Winona Root is based on two people. In *Betsy and Tacy Go Downtown* and *Winona's Pony Cart,* Maud's childhood friend Beulah Hunt was the model for Winona. The Winona Root we encounter in the high school books, however, was based on Maud's high school friend Mary Eleanor Johnson, known as "El."

Another exception is the character Joe Willard, who is based on Maud's husband, Delos Wheeler Lovelace. In real life, Delos did not attend Mankato High School with Maud. He was two years Maud's junior, and the two didn't meet until after high school. But as Maud said, "Delos came into my life much later than Joe Willard came into Betsy's, and yet he is Joe Willard to the life." This is because Maud asked her husband to give her a description of his boyhood. She then gave his history to Joe.

Maud eventually donated her high school scrapbook and many photographs to the Blue Earth County Historical Society in Mankato, where they still reside today. But she destroyed her diaries sometime after she had finished writing the Betsy-Tacy books, in the late 1950s. We can't be sure why, but we do know that, as Maud confessed once in an interview, they "were full of boys, boys, boys." She may not have felt comfortable about bequeathing them to posterity!

Maud Hart Lovelace died on March 11, 1980. But her legacy lives on in the beloved series she created and in her legions of fans, many of whom are members of the Betsy-Tacy Society and the Maud Hart Lovelace Society. For more information, write to:

The Betsy-Tacy Society
c/o BECHS
415 Cherry Street
Mankato, MN 56001

The Maud Hart Lovelace Society
Fifty 94th Circle NW, # 201
Minneapolis, MN 55448

Murmuring Lake Inn, where the Rays vacation, is based on Point Pleasant Inn at Madison Lake, Minnesota. There is an inn called Point Pleasant on the same site today, although it's not the same one.

Maud's older sister, Kathleen, at the lake.

About *Betsy Was a Junior*

THE PERIOD from 1908 TO 1909, which corresponds to the account of Betsy Ray's junior year in *Betsy Was a Junior*, was an eventful one in Maud's life. As is the case with all of the Betsy-Tacy books, much that happened to Maud made its way into the story—although at least one major event did not.

Betsy Was a Junior opens at the end of an idyllic summer spent by the Rays at Murmuring Lake. But the summer of 1908 was not quite as idyllic for Maud or her friends. A typhoid epidemic caused by contaminated water struck Mankato in June. The situation was so serious that the head of the public works board was forced to resign and the city engineer was removed from office, accused of dereliction of duty.

Maud's family, vacationing at Madison Lake, was far enough away from Mankato to be relatively safe. But several of Maud's friends and their families were affected: Mildred Oleson (Irma) and her parents, Bick's (Tacy's) father, and Marney's (Carney's) father were struck with the fever. Fortunately, they all survived. But Paul Ford (Dennie) lost his father, and Tom Fox (Tom Slade) lost his mother—a blow to the Harts, who had always been close to the Fox family.

Although the typhoid epidemic is not mentioned in the story, it may have found fictional form in the death of Cab's father and Betsy's new-found maturity at the end of the book.

Like Betsy, it appears that Maud and her crowd had lots of fun during their junior year—perhaps as a reaction to the sobering events of the summer. A happy occurrence at the beginning of the book is Tib's return to Deep Valley. Although it didn't happen in quite the same dramatic fashion, Midge Gerlach, one of Maud's closest friends, did return to Mankato after spending several years in Milwaukee. Midge instantly became one of the Crowd and was often right in the thick of things, as can be seen in many Crowd photographs of that time.

Another important factor in Crowd fun was the Willard family auto. As his fictional counterpart, Mr. Sibley, said he would do in *Heaven to Betsy*, Marney's father, W. D. Willard, purchased an auto at around this time. In an unpublished memoir, he described it as follows: "We bought our first automobile—a two-cylinder Buick, two seater, engine under the floor, right side steering, shift outside, acetylene lamps (which were very uncertain)." It cost Mr. Willard a grand total of $1,178.95.

This is the year that Maud's sister Kathleen left Mankato to attend the University of Minnesota—or

Some of the Crowd in the Willard (Sibley) family's second auto. Midge (Tib) is at the wheel with El (Winona II) at her side. Bick (Tacy) is in the backseat, at the far left.

The Oktw Deltas, from left: Midge (Tib); Mildred (Irma); Bick (Tacy); Maud (Betsy); El (Winona II); Marney (Carney); Ruth (Alice); and Tess (Katie).

the "U," as it is still called by state residents today. Like Julia, she was swept up in the sorority rush—she pledged Gamma Phi Beta in real life, not the fictional Epsilon Iota.

As in the book, sororities also became part of Maud's life. Dazzled by Kathleen's description of sororities, Maud and some of the rest of the Crowd formed Oktw Delta. (Maud used this spelling, but the word appears as "Okto" in the book.) The eight girls who joined were the same as their counterparts in the book. Maud's scrapbook contained many Oktw Delta souvenirs such as placecards from a progressive dinner and a program from a party given by eight of the boys for the sorority.

We can guess that the real-life Oktw Delta did not create such bad feeling in the high school as the fictional one did. Unlike Betsy, Maud *was* named head of the entertainment committee for the Junior-Senior banquet, and the Oktw Delta organization was not disbanded at the end of Maud's junior year. A December 1910 article in the *Mankato Free Press* reads: "The Oktw Delta club gave its annual progressive dinner last evening. . . . On Monday evening, the club gave its annual Christmas tree." Evidently, the club survived for at least another two years.

A new member of the Crowd and Betsy's love interest in the book is the silent Dave Hunt. During her

The sheet music for the "Morning Cy Barn Dance."

This cartoon of Maud was pasted in her high school scrapbook. The labels point to "naturally curly hair," "red dress," and "red socks," and the name on the dance card is "Bob."

junior year, Maud dated a boy named Robert (Bob) W. Hughes, who appears to have been the inspiration for Dave. We don't know for sure if he, too, was the strong, silent type, but it seems quite likely.

Maud also received a curling iron as a joke present at a class assembly. Pasted in her high school scrapbook is a card signed "Class 09," which reads: "Miss Maude Rosemond Palmer Hart Jones Gifford Hodson Wells Hoerr Morehart Ford Hughes Weed & etc.

Maud appears just as pleased about her Christmas furs as Betsy is in the story.

Betsy's silent beau, Dave Hunt, was based on Bob Hughes.

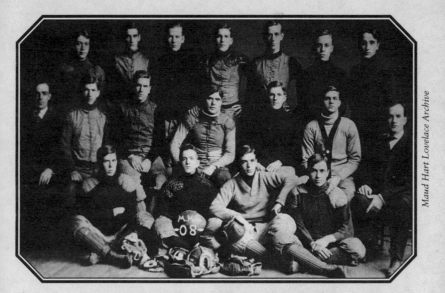

*Crowd members on the 1908 Mankato
High School Football Team pictured here include:
Bob Hughes (Dave Hunt) in the back row,
second from left; Paul Ford (Dennie) in the middle
row, second from right; and Jab Lloyd (Cab)
in the front row, third from left.*

We would like to see you curl that new crop of
whiskers now flourishing on your lily-white intellectual brow." Maud appears to have been even more
popular with boys than Betsy!

At the end of the book, Betsy reflects on the past
year of silliness and resolves to be more grown-up. We
don't know if Maud made a similar resolution, but
like Betsy, Maud certainly had a rollicking junior year.

Fictional Characters and Their Real-Life Counterparts

Betsy Ray	Maud Palmer Hart
Julia Ray	Kathleen Palmer Hart
Margaret Ray	Helen Palmer Hart
Bob Ray	Thomas Walden Hart
Jule Ray	Stella Palmer Hart
Tacy Kelly	Frances Vivian Kenney
Tib Muller	Marjorie Gerlach
E. Lloyd Harrington	James H. Baker Jr.
Dave Hunt	Robert William Hughes
Katie Kelly	Theresa Catherine Kenney
Alice Morrison	Ruth Fallie Williams
Pin	Charles Ernest (Pin) Jones
Squirrelly	Earl Elmer King
Joe Willard	Delos Wheeler Lovelace